Rose Garden Reverie

Michelle Endersby

First published by Busybird Publishing 2020

ISBN
978-1-922465-28-3 (paperback)
978-1-922465-29-0 (ebook)

Cover image: Michelle Endersby
Cover design: Busybird Publishing
Layout and typesetting: Busybird Publishing
Editor: Laura McCluskey

Busybird Publishing
2/118 Para Road
Montmorency, Victoria
Australia 3094
www.busybird.com.au

Contents

*'Teaching you to grow a garden is better than
giving you a thousand roses.'*
— **Matshona Dhliwayo**

Spring

The rusted iron gate was open, swinging gently in the breeze, but Sophia hesitated, uncertain, placing her briefcase on the uneven ground. Her chest a tight drum, her right leg wooden and her left rooted to the ground. She shifted slightly as if to go.

The Gardener then appeared before her, smiling kindly and watching her indecision.

'Good morning, and what a beautiful morning it is,' the Gardener said in a lilting accent Sophia could not place. 'Would you like to see the garden? There is always something special to see.' He indicated the way with a flourish.

'Oh, yes please, I would love to,' Sophia replied, glad to be rescued from her moment of awkwardness. Her shoulders dropped and she breathed more easily as she slipped through the gate behind the sprightly, silver-haired man with the old trousers kept up with a length of baling twine.

The garden was not visible from the road, hidden behind a majestic cypress hedge. A curved stone pathway worn smooth by many footsteps led the way in. Sophia gasped with surprise as she caught a glimpse of a most glorious rose garden stretching out before her.

'So, what is it you're looking for?' the Gardener enquired as they walked slowly side by side.

'Looking for?' she asked, perplexed.

'Everyone who comes into the rose garden is searching for something. I wonder what brought you here today?'

Sophia was not able to formulate an answer before the little man took off down the main pathway that was edged with a carpet of fragrant violets. Sophia followed him closely, not wanting to be left behind, and wishing she had worn her flat shoes. He paused when he came to a robust-looking rosebush. Its glossy green foliage was lush and abundant, and in the centre of the bush was a single plump bud. A stripe of deep magenta gave promise of a beautiful bloom inside. He stepped aside so she had a clear view.

'I think you need to see this. Be patient, watch carefully, and observe what happens.'

Without another word he backed away, and Sophia was left there alone, confused. She stood on the spot and looked intently at the rosebush. A gentle breeze ruffled the leaves, but the bud stayed still and strong. She examined the rose closer. The shiny green calyx looked like a pair of hands clasped tightly in prayer. She drew in a breath sharply as one green sepal folded back. The rose was opening.

Her heart was racing; did roses usually open this quickly? What was she witnessing? The bud gave a little shudder as if trying to shake off a cloak. There was an eagerness, but at the same time a struggle.

The rose quivered and then was still. Sophia, totally engrossed in watching the rosebud, felt disappointed and then concerned. She reached out her hand and stopped, frozen as a statue, realising the Gardener was standing beside her again.

'You can't help it to open. This is something it must do by itself,' he said seriously. 'It's a rite of passage, the rose must gather its resources and try again. To open and bloom is Nature's intended purpose when the time is right. All Winter, in the dark and cold, it has been waiting for this moment. Whilst the outer world slept, deep inside the sap was still moving, marking time, putting everything in place until the full potential was there, wound up tightly like a spring, ready to unfurl, ready to express its true nature and greatest beauty.'

The Gardener put down the two galvanised iron buckets he was holding, then with a flick of his wrists flipped them over and motioned for Sophia to join him sitting down. Out of the silence a wren started to trill and the sun came out from behind a cloud, illuminating the rosebush. The Gardener nodded and smiled, his eyes crinkling, and they both watched, transfixed, as the rosebud ever so slowly, but purposefully, opened, until before them was the most perfect rose, free of any blemish.

Tears rolled down Sophia's face, but she did not know why. She had just witnessed the most wonderful, inspiring event, so why did she suddenly feel so desolate and empty? Why was she comparing herself with the burgeoning rose bloom and feeling the heavy burden of unfulfilled potential?

The Gardener looked at her knowingly as he eased himself up to a standing position.

'Come along now,' he said encouragingly, 'I think it's time for a cup of tea.' Sophia found herself following the fascinating man down the path to a shed half covered in pink rambling roses. Sophia was not particularly tall but felt she should duck her head to go through the doorway.

When Sophia's eyes adjusted to the dim light of the potting shed, she realised she had stepped into an Aladdin's Cave. Down one end was a large wooden bench with all manner of garden tools, stacks of pots and trays of seedlings, and a selection of well-thumbed garden catalogues. Bunches of dusty dried roses hung from the rafters. Two tall glass-fronted cabinets held a collection of antiquarian leather-bound books with gold titles embossed on the spines. An ancient map of the world, yellowing and curling at the edges, was pinned to the wall above some comfortable-looking chairs draped with rich textiles embellished with rosebuds. The overall effect was both mysterious and inviting.

Sophia ensconced herself on one of the chairs but continued to stare about her in wonder. The whistling of the kettle woke her from her reverie. A tray appeared bearing a fine china teapot and cups and saucers with the Old Country Roses pattern, and a fancy filigree silver plate of rose-scented Turkish Delight dusted with icing sugar. The Gardener pulled the heavy damask drapes back from the windows to reveal a breathtaking vista of the garden, and then proceeded to pour and serve the tea. Sophia accepted a cup and saucer, and on catching a whiff of rose aroma she smiled.

'I add a modicum of dried rose petals to the teapot,' the Gardener explained secretively and offered her the plate of Turkish Delight.

Her eyes returned to the map. She saw now that roses adorned it like an illuminated manuscript and dotted lines marked out trails. She wondered what it all meant. She had one hundred and one questions to ask; her mind was buzzing. Along the base of the wall hanging in graceful calligraphy was written a quote: 'Mystery glows in the rose bed, the secret is hidden in the rose.'

Sophia thought the garden, the potting shed, and most of all the Gardener were full of secrets, but she would not question him; she just felt like basking in the glow of it all and that was enough for now. Careful not to get icing sugar everywhere, Sophia took a bite of the Turkish Delight and almost swooned with pleasure as the rich explosion of roses swept over her tastebuds. For the second time that day she felt almost overcome, but this time there were no tears; instead she felt suffused with a deep sense of peace, a feeling she couldn't recall experiencing in a very long time, if ever.

Sophia delicately replaced her cup and saucer on the tray and in doing so caught sight of her gold bracelet watch that she had been given for her twenty-first birthday.

'Gosh, is it that late?' she said, reluctantly making the journey back to reality. 'I really must be going. I've lost all track of time.'

'That is good,' the Gardener said deliberately, 'most excellent, actually. If you can forget the time, you can also forget your worries. I find that happens when you are in the rose garden. Did you enjoy your tea?' he enquired, raising his eyebrows.

'Oh yes, yes I did very much, thank you. Do you think I might be able to visit again on another day, please?' Sophia enquired hopefully, suddenly desperate for the answer to be affirmative.

'Well, let me see.' The Gardener drew out the words slowly. 'First of all, I would need to know your name.'

'I-I'm Sophia,' she stammered.

'Well, Sophia, I think you must visit again, and I could certainly do with a helping hand deadheading the roses,' the Gardener said cheekily as he rose gracefully from the low chair and escorted her to the door. The Gardener shook her hand and bowed a funny little old-fashioned bow. Sophia held his hand for a little moment, noticing the rose gold signet ring on his right little finger. It was engraved with a rose.

The following week, armed with a shallow cane basket, sharp secateurs, and a broad-brimmed hat, Sophia stepped into the first row of roses, recalling the words the Gardener had said.

'Deadheading, an unfortunate-sounding term, means removing the dead or dying blooms from the bush. It is important because it keeps the plants healthy, extends the blooming season, and keeps the rose bushes looking good. In Autumn we will let the roses form rosehips, but right now the season for blooming is still upon us.'

As the Gardener had instructed, Sophia detached each spent bloom just above where there was a sprig of five little leaves and dropped them into her basket. Feeling like someone from another time and place, she enjoyed the leisurely pace as she drifted along each row.

Careful to avoid inadvertently cutting off any new buds or blooms still in their prime, she noticed that as her focus sharpened, her visioned softened around the edges until she was viewing each bloom as a vignette; the incessant chatter in her head that was her constant companion took a break, and a feeling of peace and clarity took its place. She was aware of the fragrance of the blooms, still sweet and light, even though the vibrancy of the colours had moved to muted mauves, dusty pinks, and dirty creams. The turgor of the petals was lost, crumpled, crisping, and wilted. The satisfying *snip, snip, snip* of the secateurs and the occasional warbling of wattle birds was the accompanying soundtrack. Her back felt alternately warm and cool as clouds danced across the sky. With each bloom removed, she felt she was urging the bush into action and helping it to focus its energies. The feeling of removing the clutter and bringing the rows of shrubs into order was deeply satisfying.

With her basket almost overflowing, Sophia went down and deposited her morning's work onto the growing pile at the bottom of the garden. Feeling she had lightened the load in her basket, heart, and mind, she made her way to the potting shed.

Sophia could not recall the moment when it had first started.

It had come upon her gradually, but was slowly building to a point where she knew something had to change. A current of discontent seemed to run through her life, not caused by any one thing, she thought, but as time went on this feeling became more constant, more insidious. Perhaps it would not have reached crisis point if her mother was still alive.

Sophia's life was forever changed, forever poorer, since that morning when she received the phone call from the hospital. Still even now she would find herself reaching for the phone receiver, not forgetting that her mother was gone, but just hovering, remembering the feeling of surety that she would feel a whole lot better about the world if she could only speak to her mum. Life had lost its sparkle; a fog had descended, and sometimes this fog was so thick it was like wading through concrete. This feeling was exhausting, but Sophia knew there had to be more to life than this.

So on that morning when she had walked past the garden gate and noticed that for once it was open a crack, she knew she must investigate. The garden had always intrigued her, but she never thought that she would get a chance to go in. Thinking about this now she finds it strange because the open gate was a bolt from the blue, and suddenly it felt the most important thing in the world to be allowed in.

The Gardener appearing from out of nowhere was also a mystery. She had never seen him before, and had wondered if the garden had been abandoned. But being invited in seemed to be an important fact, that she was not trespassing, and it confirmed to her that she was on the right track and in the right place at the right time.

The Gardener was in good spirits, gently singing to himself, when Sophia opened the door to the potting shed on her next visit.

'Ah, Sophia, there you are,' he beamed. 'I have just put the kettle on!'

Sophia loved their morning ritual; the Gardener would explain what was to be done in the garden that day over a cup of rose-scented tea. But why was the Gardener so excited?

'Today, Sophia, we are staking the water shoots. Come along, let me show you,' he said as he threw a large handful of bamboo stakes and some garden ties into the wheelbarrow and led the way to the hybrid tea beds.

Sophia felt excited, too, when she saw the fresh, strong, smooth rose canes growing out from the base of the rose stems, above the bud union where the rose bush had been grafted onto root stock. Some of them were a deep burgundy and others a fresh forest green.

'During its lifespan, a rose will keep renewing itself, producing these new stems,' the Gardener explained. 'Most of the sap from the rose bush goes into them, resulting in these beautiful long canes and quality rose blooms. These stems are the future of the bush and must be protected, as they are soft and fragile when they first emerge. Help me put a bamboo stake in the ground next to each one and we'll tie them up gently.'

Sophia set to, finding the new shoots and staking them, and when they had finished and Sophia was making her way home, she felt invigorated and excited by the life force of the roses and the promise of new blooms.

On her next visit Sophia arrived at the potting shed just as fat drops of rain started to pelt down. The sprint from the bottom of the garden had left her slightly out of breath, so she stood under the verandah and leant against the rough rail post whilst she caught her breath.

She inhaled deeply and took a moment to enjoy the fresh smell of the rain. How can you describe that smell? The air seems charged with energy, and there is a sense of expectation and excitement.

Is that how the roses feel? The rain bounced off the leaves, and the bushes and buds seemed to stand taller. Only the full-headed blooms started to bow down as the weight of the raindrops built. The grass became greener and the dust settled on the paths.

Glancing down at her basket, Sophia knew she must move inside. This time her basket didn't hold the results of her deadheading. This time the basket was laden with the long stems of the finest blooms.

She rolled out a soft cloth onto the potting table and started to lay out the blooms carefully. The colour palette she had selected was soft yet luxuriant, ranging from the antique pinks of Jacques Cartier and the perfectly formed Savoy Hotel, the soft lavenders of Lagerfeld and Sterling Silver, the elegant mocha tones of Soul Sister to the palest blush of A Whiter Shade of Pale.

She ensured that the vase was spotless, had been washed with detergent and then rinsed in hot water, allowed to air dry, and was stored upside down. She removed all the foliage that would be submerged under water. Then, cutting each stem carefully under the water to avoid air pockets inhibiting the uptake of water, she arranged the blooms in a fan.

'Beautiful work Sophia,' the Gardener said, leaning back in his comfortable chair and craning his neck to get a better look at the roses Sophia was arranging, 'I can see you've done that before.'

'Well, not really or recently,' Sophia demurred. 'My grandmother used to bring roses in from the garden and put them in bud vases on the telephone table, some in a squat crystal vase on the dressing table in her bedroom, and always an arrangement in front of the mirror on the mantelpiece so she could double the appearance of the blooms.'

The Gardener watched her, smiling. 'Precious memories, Sophia, like a comforting shawl from the past you can wrap yourself in.'

I really don't know what to do, Sophia thought to herself dejectedly. *I have no idea what I am supposed to be doing with my life.*

Sophia's spirits had sunk so low that as much as she had wanted to return to the rose garden, she had struggled to get out of bed; her leaden limbs refused to budge as the heavy weight on her chest held her down and threatened to crush her.

Where was the girl who would jump out of bed early to make the most of the day? At times she felt like she was living in a dream, one of those dreams where you are trying to cross the road with cars bearing down on you and you can't move, paralysed with fear, only to be able to throw yourself into a ditch at the side of the road at the very last minute.

Just as she had resigned herself to the fact that she would not be going out today was when she smelt it. Faint at first, and then quite strong; the essence of roses, the reputed 60,000 blooms in one ounce of rose oil, was invading her nostrils and awakening every cell in her body. The fragrance filled with memories and emotions, of sunshine, bees, colour, desire, and beauty. She was on her feet; the allure of roses had broken the dark spell that was holding her.

When she described her experience to the Gardener the next day over their morning cup of tea, he was interested in what she had to say but did not appear surprised.

'Guidance is all around you, Sophia. The essence of roses you smelt was a sign that you were in the presence of the angels. Tune in to the guidance and trust your intuition, you have inner resources available to you to draw upon. You are not alone.'

What a perfect morning, not a cloud in the sky. The air so fresh and just the slightest hint of a breeze.

Sophia and the Gardener sat on the verandah, looking out to the garden in the peak of its bloom.

'This perfection is calling out for a special task,' the Gardener said finally, standing up and clapping his hands. 'Today, go into the garden, find the most perfect bloom, and bring it back here, please. Take your time and see what you can find, but only pick one rose. That is most important.'

Sophia was a little bemused by the request. Why was he so adamant that she only cut one bloom and it had to be the most perfect?

'Well, I'd better get started. How hard can this be?' she said to herself. She was only halfway down the first row when it dawned on her how difficult the task was. On the very first bush she looked at there was an exceptionally fine bud in pure white, pristine and unblemished, but it was unlikely to be the most beautiful in the garden. The next possibility was a very elegant bud on a tall stem, this one a pale pink; the rose was just starting to open so you could see the swirl of petals on top.

And so she continued, finding bloom after bloom of wondrous beauty. Finally, Sophia heard the whistle of the kettle signalling it was time for a cup of tea. She returned to the potting shed empty-handed. The Gardener looked at her quizzically up and down when she came through the door.

'Where is it? Where is this most perfect bloom?' he asked with a laugh in his voice.

'It was impossible to pick just one bloom,' Sophia said exasperatedly. 'The more I looked, the more I found. There seemed to be hundreds,' she said slumping into her chair.

'And that is exactly the point, Sophia. The more you look for beauty in the world the more you will find,' the Gardener said as he poured the tea into the cups.

Sophia had heard of the famous White Garden at Sissinghurst Castle, so was delighted when the Gardener offered to show her around his version of the White Garden.

'On a much smaller scale, of course. You'll think me very modern,' the Gardener had said. 'I call this one of my garden rooms.'

And what a room it was. Sparkling chandeliers, rich velvet curtains, a gold-leaf gilded chaise longue, and walls covered in priceless artworks could not compare with the Gardener's magnificent white garden room. Entering through an avenue of glistening Margaret Merril standards with their slightly ruffled-edge petals, the effect of all the many layers of white was astonishing. Sophia was wide-eyed in wonder, as the

Gardener warmly began to explain the features of the garden to her.

'The tall rose shrubs clothed in light green leaves and swathes of creamy white fragrant flowers way at the back and creating the walls of the room are Madame Alfred Carriere. Those perfect white rosettes packed full of petals standing out on glossy green foliage are Tranquillity.'

Sophia just loved hearing the names of the roses and she could see why the border of miniature roses at the front of the bed were called Irresistible because the blooms had the perfect rose form of a classic hybrid tea rose shrunk down to a miniature size. The Gardener had placed his most fragrant white roses near the white Lutyens garden benches so that their fragrance could be enjoyed. This included the exquisitely formed Pope John Paul II with its lemony fragrance.

'Let me show you one of my favourites,' the Gardener continued, ushering Sophia to a pearlescent ruffled rose.

'This,' he announced, 'is Devoniensis, also called the Magnolia Rose. You must smell the fragrance of it.'

Forming a natural hedge at the back of the room was a rugosa rose Blanc Double de Coubert.

'It's called the Muslin rose, and don't you think the blooms look like blousy little handkerchiefs?'

Sophia laughed, very much enjoying the tour of the white garden. Sophia and the Gardener sat on the garden bench named after the British architect Sir Edwin Lutyens and took a moment just to enjoy the ambience of the garden. The absence of colour made the garden feel restful and serene, but by no means dull. The setting was utterly enchanting and bathed in an ethereal glow. Sophia and the Gardener sat side by side not needing to say a word, and the outside world ceased to exist.

It was early in the morning, and the saying, 'The early bird catches the worm' could be extended to say, 'The early bird flicks out as much mulch as he can in his mainly unsuccessful attempts to catch a worm.'

Well, it looked like the blackbird was to be Sophia's companion for the day, and as long as it moved ahead of her and didn't mess up the paths she had already raked, she didn't mind. So intent on her raking and watching what the bird was up to, she had failed to see the stranger arrive and take up a position of ownership on the small garden bench under the climbing Pierre de Ronsard. She was so startled when she straightened up from her hunched position to find she was looking eye to eye with a bearded man in a very old-fashioned suit that she shrieked, dropped her rake, and stumbled backward.

In defiance of his age he moved deftly to catch her, then motioned for her to sit down, too. Which she did, because the shock of discovering the stranger in 'her' sanctuary was making her legs shake uncontrollably and she was worried that she would fall.

The stranger had not uttered a word, and without overtly looking at her, he was taking her in whilst still exuding his calm demeanour. There was no mistaking his relaxed confidence and manner. This was obviously not his first visit to the garden, nor the first time he had sat on that seat. Was he feeling that it was she who had invaded his sanctuary?

The stranger broke the silence first. 'The rose arbour is late to flower this year.'

His nonchalant comment was heavy with meaning. His claim on the garden obviously predated hers, and he was clearly on intimate terms with the garden and its cycles implying detailed observation and familiarity.

Sophia resumed her task of raking the paths; she was only halfway around the garden and the day was starting to heat up. As she worked her way along the Mutabilis border with its multicoloured blooms ranging from coppery yellow to pinky crimson fluttering on the bush like butterflies, she could see that the stranger was scribbling away on some pages he had taken out of a battered old leather compendium, not that she was watching what he was doing. When she rounded the final corner she noticed that he had left behind some of his papers on the bench.

She looked up and was about to call out and let him know, but he had disappeared. She briefly glanced at the papers and saw that it was poetry written out in a beautiful old-fashioned script, and signed Pierre 1555.

I send you here a wreath of blossoms blown,
And woven flowers at sunset gathered,
Another dawn had seen them ruined, and shed
Loose leaves upon the grass at random strown,
By this, their sure examples be it known
That all your beauties, now in perfect flower
Shall fade as these, and wither in an hour
Flowerlike, and brief of days, as flowers sown.
Ah, time is flying, lady-time is flying;
Nay, 'tis not time that flies but we that go,
Who in short space shall be in churchyard lying,
And of our loving parley non shall know,
Nor any man consider what we were,
Be therefore kind, my love, whiles thou art fair.

Sophia sat down on the bench where the stranger had been sitting and read the poem again, slowly this time. What were the words trying to say to her? That like the roses, beauty fades, time passes, and life is short? Once again, she was being made to think about the passage of time and the preciousness of life. Was she making the most of her precious time?

'Be therefore kind,' the poet said; she would try to be kinder to herself and in that moment, surrounded by the roses, all the paths neatly raked, Sophia smiled to herself and felt that she had spent her day in the best possible way.

Sophia and the Gardener sat opposite each other on the arbour seats under the arching canes of a rose, heavy with cascading blooms of orange fading to a pale yellow, and the air was filled with the sweet, musky fragrance of old roses. The light was beginning to fade and the shadows in the garden were lengthening.

'What is this rose?' Sophia asked, gently shaking a confetti of petals from her hair.

'Ah, what a rose, indeed. This is Crepuscule. The word means twilight in French,' the Gardener softly told Sophia, 'and twilight is the magic hour for gardeners. A time to take stock after the chores of the day are finished and before the night descends. The colours become muted, sharp edges soften, the birds head home to roost, and you can feel peace and contentedness fill every inch of your weary body.'

Sophia was feeling pleased with herself.

She didn't like seeing the life being sucked out of the delicate new growth and tiny buds of the roses by the aphids, so she had discovered that with a small flat artist's paintbrush and a jar of soapy water she could wander around the garden and paint the roses clean. She had come up with this technique herself after accidentally knocking off one of the new buds by just trying to rub the aphids off with her fingers.

Her jar of water was a swirl of green dots and she decided to take a break under the leafy Paul's Himalayan Musk Rambler that was covered in clusters of soft lilac pink flowers that faded to white, and oh, that strong musk fragrance. She was surprised to see the Gardener coming along the pathway carrying a small parcel.

'Ah, here you are,' he said, joining her on the wrought iron bench with the entwined roses design. 'Happy Birthday, Sophia.' He handed her a parcel wrapped neatly in brown paper and tied with a pale green ribbon.

'Oo, thank you, what a lovely surprise. How did you know it was my birthday?' Sophia asked incredulously.

'Oh, I know these things,' he answered. 'Please open your present, I would love to know what you think of it.'

Feeling embarrassed, Sophia started to unwrap the parcel carefully, not wanting to tear the paper or to appear greedy or impatient. When the paper finally opened she was speechless, unable to utter a word, for in front of her lay the most exquisite thing she had ever seen; a delicate scarf with an intricate pattern of roses, the folds in the petals looking like folds in the fabric, the silk like the velvety texture of the rose. Scattered rose petals made up the background of the design which was luxuriously opulent, and she could only describe it as breathtaking. It was moments before she could speak; she was so overwhelmed by the unexpected gift that seemed to belong in another world. Could anything so beautiful really exist? Would it dissolve in her hands? Was she just dreaming?

The Gardener broke the silence, saving her from having to find the words which could only be inadequate in the situation.

'I am glad you like my little gift,' he offered.

'It is the most glorious thing I have ever seen,' she said gratefully and earnestly, 'as if all the beauty of all roses has been collected and magically woven into the design. I will treasure it always, thank you so much.'

'Sophia,' the Gardener said, slowly rising. 'I know what the roses mean to you and now it doesn't matter where you are or what season it is, you can always be surrounded by roses and be comforted by their embrace.'

When Sophia looked up from admiring the precious gift, the Gardener was gone.

'Were you always interested in gardening?' Sophia asked the Gardener as they sat on the verandah, overlooking the garden after a morning of weeding.

'Weeding,' the Gardener had said earlier on, 'is one of the most satisfying jobs in a garden. You can see your progress and you are actively involved in creating order out of chaos. I love it.'

'My earliest memory,' the Gardener mused in a dreamy voice, imagining something that happened a long, long time ago. 'My earliest memory,' the Gardener repeated, 'is sitting on a grassy pathway in a rose garden laughing as rose petals shower down on me while my mother deadheads the roses above me. As a child I loved being outdoors; my biggest fear was that I wouldn't be allowed to go out in the garden and would have to stay inside. My greatest pleasure was spending time with old Jacob, the Gardener on the estate. He would give me little boy-sized tasks to do. Old Jacob saw everything in life in terms of his garden and the seasons, and taught me that the garden held the answers to any questions or problems that you had. And Old Jacob always got up early. "Dawn," he would say. "Get up at dawn, young man, and get out into the garden. That is the time of day when heaven and earth are one." As a young lad you can imagine how exciting that sounded, and still today I wake up every morning feeling excited about getting out early into the garden. Dawn,' he sighed, 'a new beginning, new opportunities, every single day.'

Sophia slipped into the garden through the archway clipped into the cypress hedge.

She inhaled the fresh smell of the hedge, and stepping into the light beyond, she felt all her cares disappear. For Sophia, the archway was a portal into another time and place, separate from her everyday existence.

Sophia felt she was a different person, too, when she was in the garden. There was no mad panic, there was nowhere she needed to be and nothing she needed to do. She never felt like she was wasting time, even when she was just wandering from one rosebush to the next, seeing what she could see; perhaps she would remove a yellowing leaf here and there, she might gently rub off some aphids from a tender new shoot, or she might deadhead a rose, remove a dead twig, or a bit of die-back. Everything was in slow motion and infinitely interesting.

Roses, in their constant cycle of change, provided endless fascination for her. From one visit to the next she would notice many differences, but even over the space of a few hours there would be subtle changes such as in the degree to which a flower had opened, which flowers the bees would be visiting, and the movement of sunshine and shadows across the garden. Sitting on the garden bench, Sophia asked, *Why do I feel so happy and contented when I am in the garden?*

Being surrounded by greenery was certainly a factor; the colour green was soothing, and seeing new growth filled her with joy and gave her hope. *Oh, I can breathe in the garden. The air seems fresher, and I can feel my chest expanding to take in slow, deep breaths of this life-enhancing atmosphere.*

Feeling perfectly safe, Sophia liked nothing more than to rest her eyes and listen to the sounds of the garden from right up close, to way out into the distance. Likewise she would explore the fragrances of the garden, creating a fragrance map in her mind, noticing the different layers of sweet, fruity, musk, and myrrh in the roses, the smell of rain in the air, and the more pungent, earthy smells of the mulch and fertiliser. Sophia never felt alone in the garden; instead she felt such a strong connection with Nature; that her world was temporarily complete.

As the light of the day faded and a slight chill could be felt in the air, Sophia got to her feet and made her way back to the archway, leaving the garden behind her, but she did not reassume her mantle of worries. Instead she felt suffused with the peace of the garden acting as a protective shield against the outside world; her steps were light, and her spirit was refreshed and renewed.

Sophia focussed on the informal vase of roses she had placed on the boardroom table, so vibrant and alive, looking out of place and exotic in this corporate setting.

Why did they have to make the air conditioning so cold? she wondered, pulling her jacket around her tighter. *Probably to keep us awake as we watch these weekly sales figures scroll down the screen.* Sophia was relieved to see that her department was on target, but apart from that she felt nothing; she had a sense of being detached and disconnected, which made it hard for her to concentrate and to feel enthused.

Sophia sank lower in her seat and tried to glance at her watch. How much longer did she have to endure this for? Someone else had joined the meeting, they were asking about the roses. Sophia brightened and sat up straighter. The roses …

'We spend a lot of time thinking about what is happening above ground in the garden,' the Gardener began, 'but underground there is a whole other world again. Above ground it is the bees who are toiling away, but underground it's the earthworms' domain.'

Sophia could tell she was in for another gardening lesson and turned round to face the Gardener.

'Tell me all about the worms,' Sophia asked, smiling.

'The worms really are the roses' ultimate companion. They do so much for them, which is why I prefer to dig using a garden fork rather than a spade where I am much more likely to cut through a worm.'

Sophia grimaced, not sure that she should have encouraged the Gardener to elaborate on this topic.

'The worms, as you can imagine,' he continued, 'create a network of tunnels through the soil and up to the surface. They aerate the soil, allow water to drain to the roots and break down organic matter, and deposit it in these tunnels where the roses have easy access for growth and a ready source of nutrients. Different types of worms live at different levels in the soil, a bit like a multi-storey building, which is why it is a good idea not to disturb your soil too much. But putting leaf litter or mulch that the worms can feed on and break down is something positive you can do for the worms, and ultimately for your roses.'

When Sophia went back to her multi-storey building that evening, she was thinking of the earthworms living in their layers.

The platform was deserted as Sophia stood waiting for the train, holding her basket of roses.

The Gardener encouraged her to gather roses to take home each Friday, and the difference it made to the ambience and feeling of homeliness in her dreary apartment was considerable.

To wake up on a Saturday morning to the fragrance and colour of blooms made Sophia feel like she was in the garden already, and gave her the same sense of peace. And as the week went on she would change the display, removing a drooping head, or putting just a single bloom on her writing desk, and sometimes just letting a scatter of petals fall in abstract patterns.

Sophia never usually looked forward to going home – she even thought that calling the place home was a misnomer – but on a Friday afternoon with a basket of lavish blooms she felt an unfamiliar cheerfulness imagining the combinations and visualising the arrangements she would create. Completing her work assignments and dreary reports in her office always felt less burdensome when she was surrounded by roses.

The recorded station message alerted her that the train was about to arrive. The train slowed to a halt and the automatic doors beeped but did not open, as no one was getting off the packed commuter train. All the seats were taken and people were standing in the aisle hanging on. But when Sophia stepped into the carriage with her roses, she felt every eye on her. She was probably younger and fitter than most of the passengers and she was carrying roses, not a baby, but suddenly five people had stood up to let her have a seat.

Feeling embarrassed, but not wanting to offend, Sophia hurriedly took a seat and mumbled a thank you. The seats around her quickly filled and the one man who had been displaced by her arrival smiled somewhat smugly as if he had won a prize. She did not know what made her do it, but her hand wavered over the roses until it rested on a striking bloom of deep magenta. She picked it up and handed it to the victor.

There was a collective sigh. Oh no, she had started something. Everyone's attention was on the roses. Sophia was glad she had prepared the roses by removing the thorns and the lower leaves.

'What are these flowers?' one man ventured to a chorus of titters.

'These are garden roses, vastly different from the roses you buy at the florist,' Sophia said with a smile.

'Oh, garden roses,' the man said, relieved. 'I'd never seen any roses like those in a shop.'

And top marks for bravery and honesty, Sophia thought as she handed out the second flower, this one a burnished copper stately bloom. The man inhaled deeply.

The woman in the smart navy suit and towering heels lent over the basket, looking at the roses adoringly and expectantly. For her, Sophia selected something unashamedly feminine, a ruffle of pink and white petals – just exquisite. As the journey continued, the scent of roses was filling the compartment more and more. A reserved older lady sat in the corner; hands clasped on her lap. Glancing out of the corner of her eyes she was taking in the roses, trying not to be seen. Sophia's hand fluttered over the roses and came to rest on the dark red rose in the centre of the bunch. She picked it up and could not resist smelling the deep fruity fragrance, the aroma of old-world roses. She gazed down into the centre of deeply swirling petals and then passed it over to the lady in the corner. Sophia watched her face flush slightly and then saw her eyes fill with moisture, a single tear rolling down her lined cheek and dropping like an offering onto the seductive bloom. Had the red rose picked for her stirred the memories of a lost love? The train picked up speed for the express part of the journey and the man sitting opposite Sophia, who had been taking in the whole saga, asked, 'Do you think I may possibly take these home for my mother?' pointing to a stem of a yellow floribunda rose with multiple blooms.

'Yes, of course,' Sophia said.

Summer

A hot northerly wind was swirling up dust as the full heads of the rose blooms nodded and drooped. The Gardener was busying himself with a watering can, a terracotta bowl, and some large stones.

'We're not going to water in the heat of the day, are we?' Sophia asked, having already had a long discussion with the Gardener about the best time of day to water: early in the morning, don't send your roses to bed wet, water at the base of the plant, don't wet the leaves if they won't dry before nightfall, water deeply, mulch to retain moisture, and enrich sandy soils to hold more moisture.

'This water is not for the roses,' the Gardener explained. 'Come down to the heritage border with me and I will show you what I'm doing. On a day like this I need to look after my bees.'

'I didn't know you had bees,' Sophia stated, surprised.

'You've seen the bees in the garden,' the Gardener answered.

'Yes, but I didn't know you have a hive.' she said.

'I don't have a hive. The bees have a hive somewhere, I don't know where,' he said looking around dreamily. 'I call them my bees because they live in my garden and I feel responsible for them, and want to make sure they have everything they need. And on a hot day like this, bees need water to keep the hive cool. Some bees will be out looking for water. They will drink some and take it back to the hive and pass it over to one of the bees in the hive, and then that bee will spread a layer of water over the cells in the hive where the eggs and the larvae are. Then the other bees in the hive will make an air current flow through the hive by flapping their wings, and as the water evaporates it will cool the air. That's why I need to leave water out for my bees.'

Sophia watched in silence as he filled the terracotta bowl with smooth river pebbles and filled it up with water.

'Now, it is most important that we put this in a shady spot otherwise the pebbles will heat up too much. I want the bees to be able to land on the stones and drink without falling in and drowning, and in time I want the bowl and rocks to grow slimy with algae because that helps the bees sniff out the water. If I put out tap water with chlorine or other chemicals in it the bees don't always recognise it as a water source, but algae is what past generations of bees have known a water source to smell like. Sophia, there is so much we can learn from bees, but that is a topic for another day.'

It had taken a long time to get dark, and the warmth from a day bathed in sunshine remained within the walls of the garden.

Above the tall hedge the round full moon peeked over and appeared to pull itself up into the dark velvety sky. A chorus of cicadas accompanied the planets ascent into the dome of the sky, and soon the glimmering moonlight made the avenues of white roses glow, and with their beauty in the spotlight their fragrance, too, appeared to be more noticeable, and the night-time garden was filled with magic.

Sophia, sitting on the comfortable bench on the verandah surveyed the scene as if the curtains of a theatre had parted, the houselights had dimmed, and all you could see was a row of elegant beings waiting and watching back. There was an air of expectancy and excitement, so Sophia was not altogether surprised when someone entered the scene from stage left. The confident footsteps crunched on the gravel slowly but determinedly. They appeared to be no stranger to the garden, walking straight along the pathway as if they had done so many times before; no, as if it was their garden.

Now Sophia was not sure what she should do; strangely, she wasn't frightened. In fact, ever since she first spotted the stranger she had felt an incredible sense of peace, calm, and an alertness. This feeling was most foreign to her, but she thought if she could feel like this again, or even just know that it was possible to feel like this, then her life would be transformed and all that ailed her would cease to exist. She thought she might startle the visitor if she spoke or moved; he would not be expecting someone to be sitting in the shadows late at night. So, she did not speak and she did not move; she just sat there calmly, watching.

He came to a fork in the pathway and paused for a moment. He took the pathway on the right and strode straight towards the potting shed.

'Sophia,' he said warmly, as if he had known her all her life, 'isn't there something magical about moonlight?'

'Oh, there certainly is. I can't seem to drag myself away, but I really must head off home,' Sophia answered.

'Yes, I'm leaving now, too. I'll lead the way' he offered graciously.

Sophia rose from the bench and followed along in the direction of the wooden gate. She turned back to latch the gate, wondering if her companion was going to be catching the train, too, but when she looked around there was no one there; only the friendly face of the moon to see her out of the garden.

Sophia and the Gardener were enjoying their morning cup of tea and discussing the tasks for the day. It was one of those days when the early morning air seemed fresher than usual, and you felt glad to be alive.

'I believe you met my son,' the Gardener stated after they had been sitting silently for a moment.

'Your son?' Sophia asked wide-eyed. 'That was your son in the garden the other night? I did not know you had a son. We didn't say much but he had such a calming presence, and I immediately felt like I had known him always. He seemed to know me, too.'

'Yes, that's Michael. Sometimes we see him in the garden.'

'Please tell me about him. What does he do?' Sophia asked curiously.

'Hmm, how can I explain what Michael does?' the Gardener began hesitantly. 'On the job front he is quite in his own realm. He works in Communications and Security. He's always looking out for people, has their best interests at heart. He tells me he spends quite lot of time trying to catch people's attention, but they rarely pay heed to what he has to say. Which is a shame; he's a wise lad, my son.'

Sophia smiled at how proud the Gardener was of his son. She hoped she would see him again.

Sophia was exhausted when she arrived in the garden that afternoon.

She chose to sit in the central gazebo which had alternating white Sea Foam and Pinkie climbers, making it look like an old-fashioned fairground carousel. Breathing in the sweet fragrance of the roses, she found that she could hardly keep her eyes open. She had worked late into the night tapping away on the computer on a report only to find that when she clicked submit nothing happened. She had clicked back to the form she had spent hours filling in only to find it was blank, and she had to start again.

However, the tiredness she felt was much more than just from a late and frustrating night spent hunched over the keyboard. Sophia felt not only a tiredness behind her eyes, but deep into her bones, and even deeper into her heart and soul; a tiredness that was not appropriate for someone her age. A tiredness brought about by too long swimming against the tide, from struggling to fit into a world that did not seem right for her, and a feeling of being overwhelmed by too much happening around her.

The Gardener, who must have observed her low mood and lower energy level, joined her in the gazebo with an old book bound in red leather and a magnificent bunch of medium pink Zephirine Drouhin blooms that had a strong damask fragrance.

'So, Sophia, what is it that is troubling you?' the Gardener asked.

'Oh, I don't know,' Sophia said. It was even an effort for her to draw out the words. 'I can't explain it, I just have this feeling of discontent.' Her words started to flow more freely. 'I feel like I have headed off down the wrong track and I don't know how to turn things around.'

'Tell me more,' the Gardener said gently.

'This feeling has been creeping up on me for so long, I can't even remember when it first started happening, but sometimes I can't even remember when there was a time when I felt really happy. Deep down I have a sense that once upon a time life was perfect, everything was right in my world, and I just didn't realise it or appreciate it. And now I know that things can never be that way again and it fills me with sadness.' Sophia sighed deeply.

'Why didn't you realise back then that things were good in your life? What else was going on that stopped you from paying attention?' the Gardener asked as she searched for her next thought.

'That's the really sad part. Nothing out of the ordinary was happening, I was just caught up in the busy-ness of everyday living and didn't stop to appreciate the precious gift of life.' Sophia lamented.

'Well, things don't have to stay the same as they are now. It is never too late to make a new start, Sophia. And sometimes all it takes is to pay attention to what is happening in your life right now and find the joy in everyday miracles. Like the roses.'

The Gardener then handed Sophia an amazing pink bloom, its soft petals folded and curved so you could look down deep into the rose. The petals were not tightly furled, just gently touching each other.

'Take a moment to get to know the rose,' the Gardener began in his soft, gentle voice. 'Imagine that you are small enough to step inside the bloom. Work out how you might explore the passageways, and find a place where you can sit down or lie down and rest. Make yourself comfortable, close your eyes, and be supported by the rose. Be enveloped by the petals, feel safe and protected. Rest within the rose for as long as you like, and then you will emerge rested, refreshed, rejuvenated, and renewed.'

Sophia didn't know how long she had rested there, imagining that she was inside the rose, but when she opened her eyes at last she had to admit that she felt much better.

'I must be hearing things,' Sophia mumbled to herself, standing stock-still on the garden path, ears straining.

Silence.

Then a dry leaf scuttled along in front of her, the only sound to be heard. It came again, clear and unmistakable, the lilting sound of a harp. Now it was her eyes that strained as she scanned the garden to see where the beautiful music was coming from, hardly daring to move, not wanting to break the spell. Sunlight was catching on something white down in the hollow near the avenue of weeping standards. Blinking her eyes and shifting her weight to her right foot she could just see the outline of a man's shirt and yes, yes it was him; the Gardener's son, Michael, bathed in pure white light playing the harp.

Placing her tools gently on the ground, she tiptoed across the grassed area and slipped onto the bench in the dappled shade of the Gingko tree, where she could watch him play unnoticed. She didn't just hear the wondrous music rippling out from the harp, she could feel it pulsating deep inside her until it felt that she was part of the music and that she was sending it out as much as receiving it. With a final arpeggio of notes, the harpist placed both hands on the strings, and although the sound of the harp could no longer be heard, Sophia found that she could still feel the vibrations resonating around and through her.

She sat there for a few minutes, maybe longer, and then she slowly opened her eyes. To her great surprise, she found that she was alone in the garden. Moving in slow motion because that was all she was capable of, she glided over to where the harpist had been playing. The gravel path looked as if it had been raked smooth, and on the bench where he had been sitting was just a single white feather.

Sophia sat down and picked up the feather. She wondered where Michael had gone; she would have liked to hear more of his playing and to speak to him. Sophia had not spent much time in this part of the garden, and the rose bed surrounding the bench she was sitting on had a very pretty selection of roses. Three varieties were intermingled; there was a mauve with ruffled petals, another exhibited a subtle spectrum of white from soft pearl through to apricot at the centre, and the third ranged from white to soft pink with globular peony-shaped flowers. And oh, what a fragrance. She could detect lemon, elderflowers, and raspberries. It was out of this world.

With the feather she still had in her hand, Sophia brushed back the layer of mulch that obscured the nameplates for the roses. The mauve was Angel Face, the pearl rose was Guardian Angel, and the soft pink delight was Earth Angel.

'A bed of angel roses,' Sophia sighed, 'simply divine.'

As Sophia walked through the garden that morning she was battered by a hot northerly wind, the sun a red fiery orb peeking through a dirty grey haze. The smell of burning gum leaves was in the air, and a fire engine siren could be heard way off in the distance. The currawongs were making pathetic cries as they staggered around under the trees, opening and shutting their beaks trying to cool down.

Sophia noted gratefully that the bird baths had been filled and the splatters of water around them showed they were being put to good use. She walked past rose bushes with tender green buds bowing right down to the ground and delicate new burgundy foliage limp and burnt to a deep purple crisp.

'What a scorcher out there,' Sophia sighed, dropping her bag on the floor and sinking down onto one of the low chairs in the cool and dim interior of the potting shed. The Gardener was busy making his pot of rose tea.

'Tea is the most refreshing drink even in the hot weather,' he said, handing Sophia a cup and saucer.

'How will the roses ever survive this heat?' Sophia asked. 'I can hardly believe what I have just seen out in the garden.'

'I gave the roses a deep soaking last night, giving them a chance to absorb the water into their tissues. They are wilting now, but that limits further water loss by reducing the surface area exposed to the drying rays of the sun. And you will be surprised to see how a well-hydrated plant recovers as the temperature cools down, especially in the coolness of the following morning where those plants will be standing up tall again ready for the new day. We will have some work trimming off some burnt foliage, but for now that is protecting the canes and leaves further inside the bush from burning. Early this morning I harvested all the rosebuds that had their sepals folded back and brought them inside. I removed the lower foliage and recut their stems under water and I am confident that they will all open up over the next few days. Take a look!'

Sophia was amazed to see the Gardener's cut crystal vases filled with colourful rosebuds all beginning to open.

'They all would have shrivelled up and died if we left them out on the bushes in this heat, and now we get to enjoy them,' he said.

'It's like you have brought the garden inside,' Sophia enthused, no longer feeling downhearted by the harshness of the weather. 'But what about our tasks for today?' she asked the Gardener, wondering if she had the energy to lift herself out of her comfortable seat and head back into the heat.

'No, there's nothing to be done today except relax, read a book, have a doze, or perhaps listen to some music,' he said.

Sophia couldn't recall seeing it before, but in the far corner of the shed was an HMV gramophone complete with a shiny gold sound horn. The Gardener shuffled through some old 78 records and pulled one carefully from its paper sleeve. He wound the handle and then said, 'Close your eyes and let this wash over you as you imagine the garden in full bloom on a beautiful Spring day. Claude Debussy knew about being pleasantly lost in one's thoughts. This is *Reverie.'*

Sophia woke with a start and, suddenly alert, sprang to her feet and threw open the curtains of her bedroom. She tugged at the window she rarely opened, and through a small crack took a deep breath. Yes, she could smell something in the air; now, what was it? The whiff of possibility. Yes, that was what it was!

Feeling excited by the unfamiliar lightness of her mood and the sense of expectation in the air, she flicked through the coat hangers in her wardrobe, bypassing her gardening clothes and stopped abruptly when her hand rested on the cool, smooth texture of a silk dress with a beautiful floral print. She pulled it out.

'Perfect,' she murmured, moving as if in a dream. On top of the wardrobe was a sunhat in fine straw with a wide brim. She took that with her into the kitchen where a vase of roses from the garden awaited. With fine florist wire she attached sprays of roses just beginning to open all around the base of the crown of the hat and fastened a ribbon of palest blush to match the dress.

She was admiring her creation as she rode along in the bus when she noticed her stop whizz by. Reaching up, she pulled the cord for the next stop. Of course, she could walk back from there; it was not too hot yet, and she had her hat. But perhaps she could find a way to enter the garden from the North side, never having entered the garden anywhere except via the small gate she had found that first day.

The bus slowed to a stop and she alighted down the back stairs. She let it zoom off before she put on her hat and turned around to take in her surroundings. Crossing over the road she could see a thick and wild hedge; no man or beast could pass through. The wooden door was well hidden under an archway of tiny, perfect, pale-pink Cécile Brünner roses. The brass door handle in the rounded shape of a centifolia rose was green with age but turned smoothly, and the door opened with a creak but little resistance. Closing it securely behind her, she stepped into the dappled sunlight reminiscent of an Emanuel Phillips Fox painting. A short stroll found her at the start of what she fondly called The Grand Promenade.

This avenue of standard roses afforded a view of the whole garden sweeping down to the central gazebo, onto the grassed area near the stream, and beyond to the Lorraine Lee hedge that flowered for eleven months of the year, the Gardener had once told her.

But today it was not the view of the garden that commanded her attention, for in front of her, laid out like a perfect diorama, there appeared to be a garden party in full swing. Ladies holding parasols were promenading along the pathways, a lavish picnic was set out on the grass, and a string quartet began to play. Sophia could not believe how alive and cheerful the garden looked. She did not waste time wondering why she had not been told that the event was happening. She just entered into the spirit of it.

A young man was making his way eagerly towards her from across the lawn. He looked remarkably familiar, but at the same time she had no idea at all who the lad was.

'So glad you could be here, Sophia,' he said, kissing her lightly on the cheek, 'and your hat looks lovely.' A faint blush coloured his cheeks.

'I'm delighted to be here,' Sophia said, acting as if she knew what was going on. 'The garden looks magical today,' she breathed, 'as if this is how it is meant to be.'

'Exactly,' the young man said, 'beauty and joy must be shared and released out into the world, beauty and joy expand when they are shared.'

What a very strange expression, she thought to herself, *but a lovely sentiment.* At that point three ladies with the parasols bustled along, and the young man bowed slightly to Sophia and went over to greet them. He gave Sophia a friendly wave and she noticed the glint of rose gold on his right hand.

Sophia wondered how she had managed to step back in time to be here. 'Time means nothing in the garden,' the Gardener had often told her.

'The Gardener,' she said to herself, 'that had to be him.'

Sophia looked around her for the best spot to survey the spectacle opting for a spot out of the sun as it was now beginning to heat up. She hovered in the shadows, curious about the three ladies, but too shy to approach them. Two of the ladies had pulled up wicker chairs on the terrace and were sitting between the urns of red roses. One was dressed in lavender, the other in powder blue, their broad-brimmed hats protecting their peaches-and-cream complexions. The third lady, also in an ankle-length dress, hers the palest buttery yellow, was standing and holding a parasol.

Sophia strained her ears, trying to hear what they were talking about, but they were just too far away. The ladies were speaking very softly but it was the way they were talking and listening to each other that made Sophia feel like an interloper. But the more she felt like an outsider, the more she wanted to be included. The lady in yellow turned around, and as if just noticing her lingering spoke out.

'Come over and join us, Sophia, there's more chairs here.'

Sophia could not believe her luck; not only being invited to sit with them, but they seemed to know her, too.

'You know my name, but I don't know yours.' She looked at each of the faces in turn.

'Oh, you *do* know us, you just need to be reminded,' the lady in yellow explained, nodding encouragingly. 'I'm Joy,' she said with a little curtsey.

'Hope,' the lady in blue added.

The lady in lavender rose elegantly and, offering Sophia a gloved hand, said, 'I'm Patience,' and smiled so warmly and genuinely that Sophia felt tears pricking her eyes.

'Joy, Hope, and Patience,' Sophia repeated the virtue names to herself, not only so she would remember their names, but also reflecting on what Joy had said.

'You do know us, you just need to be reminded.'

Joy, Hope, and Patience. *Mmm*, she thought to herself, *I would like to know them better.*

Sophia floated the rose embroidered shawl and a cushion onto the soft green grass and, feeling a little embarrassed and unsure, lay down in the garden.

At eye level the blades of grass looked huge, each a tall tree towering overhead. An ant tried unsuccessfully to climb up to the very top, but his tiny weight pulled the blade down and he hopped off and went on his way. Sophia laid back with her hands behind her head. The wispy clouds were a clip of merino wool stretching out across the sky. They did not get very far, changing shape and fading into nothingness. The temporary nature of the clouds intrigued her, and she imagined attaching a worry to each of the clouds and watching it dissolve into the blue sky. When no more worries came to mind, her heavy eyelids drooped, and she fell into the deep sleep that only comes on a Summer afternoon when you have no pressing obligations.

Sophia knew she was still asleep; she was in that cosy place just before you begin to wake up. Her eyes were closed firmly, and her breathing was deep and even. She did not want to awaken yet; she sensed that she had just dreamed something, or there was something else she needed to see. In this dream state, her vision was hazy as if looking through an unwashed window.

Then she saw him, the Gardener, walking slowly along the garden path. He was leading a group of people, young and old. He stopped when he got to the garden gate and farewelled each person, handing them a small envelope that they opened, read the card inside, nodded, and smiled. Some shook his hand, others embraced him.

Suddenly Sophia was startled and she nearly opened her eyes to see things more clearly because there at the back of the group, smiling and walking confidently, she could see herself. So strange to be observing herself as if she were a stranger, but she lay still, hardly daring to breathe and fearing she would awaken before she found out what was in the envelope.

At last it was her turn; she was no longer the observer. The Gardener smiling at her as he always did, handed her the envelope. With trembling fingers, she extracted the card that had just one word, chosen just for her.

Sophia read the word and felt it filling her heart. She looked up to acknowledge the Gardener, but she was there by herself. However, she did not feel alone.

The Gardener often spoke of having different garden rooms, and there was one section of the garden that was hugely different. In fact, it was quite mysterious. You entered through a roughly hewn wooden door and a pathway snaked in and out, and on either side of the path were hedges of wild roses either covered in simple pale pink five-petal flowers, or laden with burnished ruby rose hips depending on the season. Suddenly, quite unexpectedly, you would turn around a corner to find a small alcove with a garden seat in front of a decorative trellis displaying pink and yellow Masquerade roses.

'This garden feels so different, please tell me about it,' Sophia asked the Gardener one day when they were trimming the roses back from the pathway.

'How does it feel different, Sophia?' the Gardener asked fielding the question back at her.

'Well you never know what to expect as you walk along the paths, so it feels a bit exciting and adventurous. And even though I know what I will find each time I come to the alcoves, it always feels like a surprise. And then the end of the pathways seem to disappear, and you find yourself walking on the grass between the rose hedges.'

'Yes,' the Gardener said, 'it is good spending time in a garden of mystery. When we travel off the well-beaten track, we awaken ourselves to possibilities, and we need to embrace the unfamiliar to grow and fulfil our highest potential. Life is not always predictable and cannot always be carefully planned. Unexpected events occur, and it is how we respond to the unexpected that determines our level of happiness and whether we thrive or merely survive.'

Sophia and the Gardener sat for a while quietly in one of the secret alcoves before collecting their tools and heading back for the day. The Gardener walked off in the opposite direction to which they had come and waited for Sophia to catch up before holding up some of the rose canes for her to duck under. The pair were instantly at the back door of the potting shed, with Sophia shaking her head in disbelief.

Somehow you could tell when most severe heat of Summer was over, as each day Autumn moved a little closer. Still, the sun could feel quite hot and the nights were mild.

The garden seemed to be enjoying the gentler conditions and the abundant new growth that clothed the rose bushes wasn't being burnt to a crisp, so it looked lush and clean. The blooms, which had been smaller in the hottest periods of the season as if they had been forced to develop too quickly and had been unable to reach their full size, were now increasing in size nicely. Sophia cut roses for the Gardener to enjoy in the potting shed, and also took a large basket home each week, and still she continued with the dead heading. Sophia marvelled at the generosity of a plant which, the more you took from it, the more it would give back.

'Time to get the roses ready for their Autumn flush, Sophia,' the Gardener announced brightly when she poked her head into the shed to wish him a good morning.

'Oh really, what do we need to do?' Sophia asked, wondering what more could be done when the roses seemed to be happily plodding along.

'In Winter when we prune the roses, we take the bushes down by two thirds, and in Summer we do a light prune taking just one third of the bush,' he explained laughing at Sophia's reaction.

'We prune in Summer? I thought that was just something you did in Winter,' she stated incredulously.

'Well, the Summer prune that happens in the third month of the season is a little bit different, but it's lots of fun. You will enjoy it,' the Gardener said enthusiastically. 'For a start, you don't have to do it all in one go, so it's a more leisurely process and you have already been making a start when you have been cutting nice long stems on the roses you bring inside, and also when you are dead-heading. The leaves protect the stems from sunburn, so we still like to keep the bushes well clothed in case we get a major hot day or two. So, let us go out and I will show you the joys of Summer pruning.'

The Gardener and Sophia stood in front of a rose with coppery blooms.

'Ah, the Opportunity rose. I first like to look for any blind shoots,' the Gardener said, starting his demonstration.

'Blind shoots?' Sophia asked, puzzled. 'What are blind shoots?'

'Here's one,' the Gardener said showing her a rose stem that had no bud at the end of the stem, as if the rose had got so far in its development and then stalled. 'These stems are never going to produce flowers, so we cut them down to an outward facing bud eye that shows promise. At the same time, look out for leggy and spindly growth and trim that down by one third …,'

'To an outward facing bud eye,' they chorused together.

And so the Summer pruning began.

The Gardener was right, Sophia did enjoy it. Neatening the bushes, removing unproductive stems, and finding potential and promise. It was very satisfying work.

Work? Sophia questioned herself. *I have not worked for one day in this garden, I have loved every minute of it. It has been much more like play than work, and I would rather be playing with roses any day.*

After a few hours out in the sun, Sophia looked around for the Gardener but he was nowhere to be seen, so she wheeled her barrow up to the potting shed.

'Surely it must be time for a cup of tea?'

'Yes, it is time for tea, but not for us,' the Gardener said as he mixed up watering cans of liquid fertiliser at the water tank. 'As we take away from the bush, we must give back, so after we do the Summer prune we give them their Summer feed. And it is important to keep hydrated out in the garden, so I have made some rose iced tea for you,' he said pointing to a thermos flask in a basket. 'Please help yourself and remind me to write out the recipe for you later.'

Sophia paused as she entered the grand avenue of the garden and bent down to remove her shoes so she could stand barefoot on the grass. She consciously moved her focus to where her feet made contact with the ground, taking a moment to adjust her posture so that her weight was balanced evenly between her heels and her toes. She then started to walk slowly, maintaining her awareness of what she could see, hear, and smell around her.

After a few minutes she changed the focus to the movement of her body as she walked, and the feel of her feet as they were caressed by the soft and spongy grass. Sophia continued her walking meditation for a few moments until she reached one of the benches and took a seat. She sat there for a little while, breathing slowly and evenly, feeling calm, contented, and strongly connected to the earth.

Moving trance-like, she slipped her feet back into her shoes and meandered to the side gate. There was no need for her to spend any more time in the garden now. She was refreshed and enlivened and ready to get on with the rest of her day.

Autumn

The transition between Summer and Autumn can be quite subtle, but Sophia sensed it in the crispness of the air that morning as she walked into the garden.

She went through the rusted gate and up the same path she had walked with the Gardener on her very first day in the garden. Turning the corner, she could still see a lot of colour in the garden. Not like the full first flush of blooms that had peaked in Spring, but there was an intensity in the hue of the blooms that she hadn't noticed in the heat of Summer when the blooms developed quickly and faded just as swiftly. Sophia could also see a hint of colour in the leaves of the surrounding liquidambar trees signalling the change of season.

When Sophia entered the potting shed that morning, the aroma of freshly-brewed coffee filled the air, and on the lace tablecloth a crystal bowl filled with exotic-looking blooms took centre stage alongside a plate of coffee scroll biscuits.

'Coffee?' Sophia asked, shaking her head and trying to make sense of why the morning routine of pots of tea had altered. Coffee, which she associated with throwaway cups and racing commuters nursing their heart starters, had no place in the world of the Gardener. Still, he looked like an expert as he filled the stovetop stainless-steel coffee percolator and set it on the gas. The gurgling sound as the steam made its way through the coffee grounds signalled it was time to pour the dark liquid into the tiny gold-rimmed espresso cups.

Studying the perfectly formed hybrid tea roses, Sophia observed that they were the colour of latte, mocha, and cocoa, and had deep espresso centres, while the faded outer petals were a creamy milk chocolate.

'Julia's rose,' the Gardener finally said, 'probably the best-known coffee-coloured rose, a popular choice for weddings,' he added. 'These ones are Soul Sister, also known as Koko Loko.'

'Stunning roses,' Sophia agreed, 'but do we really need to honour them by drinking coffee?'

'Well, I thought you would find this interesting,' he said. 'The coffee grounds are one of the secrets behind these beautiful roses. Whenever we cut off a bloom or prune the roses, we are taking away nutrients from the bushes, and coffee grounds are one of the ways we can give back to the rose.'

'*Rosa gigantea*,' the Gardener sighed after a long period of silence. In his hands he held a small pot reverently. Sophia had to look twice to see the tiniest shoot pushing its head through the soil.

'*Rosa gigantea*,' the Gardener said again, his voice full of admiration and awe, 'comes from the foothills of the Himalayas and can grow 50 feet in height. It is as if it has looked up to those high and magnificent snow-capped peaks and slowly and steadily began its ascent. But this is how they start out, just the tiniest of shoots, so tiny they have no room for doubt. Dream big, Sophia. Set your sights on high peaks and start climbing. Dream big.'

As Autumn leaves drifted down lazily to form a natural layer of mulch under the roses, the final blooms for the season reached up towards the sun.

Sophia and the Gardener stood below these high blooms and, looking up, were treated to a magnificent sight. The sun shone through the translucent petals like rays through a stained glass window. The tiny veins were prominent, giving a sense that the blooms were more real, more alive, somewhat human in nature.

'Autumn is a delicious time in the rose garden,' the Gardener had explained. 'You can almost see Nature slowing down, drawing inwards, but at the same time it looks like the rose bushes have saved their most beautiful blooms until the end as if they know that the time of dormancy is soon to be upon them, there is great beauty in the temporary and the ephemeral which is why we must revel in change and impermanency knowing that we can't have things stay the same always, and that trusting in the flow and cycle of life will allow us to avoid great sadness and disappointment.'

Sophia was sitting in the garden one afternoon and thinking just how lucky she was to have a job where she could work her own hours, and apart from her weekly check-in meetings, she could work wherever and whenever she desired.

How many people get to do that? She would never have been able to spend so much time in the garden if she had a nine-to-five job. But her job didn't inspire her or excite her, whereas spending time in the garden enriched her life.

However, sometimes when she was working she could feel subtle changes in the way she saw and approached her job. Her data entry was like planting seeds and her reports she wrote were the harvest she reaped.

Engrossed in a thick sheaf of papers, the Gardener, turned slightly as Sophia walked in to deposit her basket and paraphernalia from her morning's work. He handed her a thick piece of yellowing parchment paper.

'What do you make of this?' he asked. Written in bold and beautiful calligraphy she read the words out loud.

'Mystery glows in the rose bed, the secret is hidden in the rose.'

She remembered that this was the quote on the wall hanging she had noticed on the first day she had visited the garden. What indeed did she make of it? Was this a clue from an ancient treasure hunt? What could be hidden in the rose?

'I really don't know what to make of it. Where did it come from?' she asked.

'It was written in the 12th century by a Persian poet by the name of Farid Uddin Attar,' the Gardener explained.

'Attar, as in *attar of roses*?' she exclaimed.

'Exactly. I believe Attar was a pen name he took for his occupation which meant herbalist, druggist, perfumer, or alchemist, but I also think it is possible that the exquisite rose oil was named after him. The Persians were wild about roses, they saw rose gardens as a symbol of heaven. The mystery, I believe, has something to do with finding an experience of heaven whilst still on earth. If the secret lies in the rose, then I must find out what it is, and I thought perhaps you, Sophia, could help me. I would love to know what you come up with.'

On her next visit Sophia sat at the tiny desk under the window. A vase of fragrant roses was positioned in front of her and she sipped slowly on a cup of the rose tea. A few rose petals fell from the blooms onto her brand-new notebook whose soft cover reminded her of the texture of rose petals, and next to that sat a pile of reference books. She pondered the phrase for a moment and then set to work looking for clues to puzzle it out.

She started to write in pencil in her looping script, feeling bold about what she wrote because it was in pencil and it could easily be rubbed out if needs be.

Mystery - a matter that remains unexplained.
Enigma, puzzle, secret, riddle, conundrum.

She continued writing as if in a trance.

Mystery glows in the rose bed, the secret is
hidden in the rose.

Mystery glows in the rose bed, the secret is
hidden in the rose.

Mystery glows in the rose bed, the secret is
hidden in the rose.

Over and over she wrote out the phrase, like a mantra, an incantation, hoping that these words written nine centuries earlier would release a clue, just the slightest hint to their meaning, or at least an idea of where to investigate.

'Well, let me break it down' she mused.

Mystery - a matter that remains unexplained

Glows - send out light & heat without flame.

Glowing - expressing great praise.

Noun: gleam, shine, glimmer, radiance, light.

Rose bed - bed, sleeping, not awake, not
aware, not conscious.

The secret is hidden in the rose.

Secret - kept from the knowledge of most people.

Hidden - concealed, secret, unseen, out of sight, camouflaged, disguised.

A miracle - an event so extraordinary that it is attributed to supernatural causes.

Supernatural - not able to be explained by the laws of Nature.

Nature - the physical world with all its features and living things.

Sophia underlined some words in the phrase. She closed her eyes, her breathing was unsteady. She felt she was on the cusp of discovering something. If this is not about living things in the physical world, what world could it be referring to? She recalled having heard the phrase 'the great unseen', but was not sure what it meant.

But then she thought back to her first day in the garden and seeing that rose open up before her as if unseen forces were at work. Suddenly Sophia was aware of the feeling of her feet on the ground beneath the table where she sat. Her feet felt warm in her shoes; she could feel the softness of her socks against her skin and the pressure of where the soles of her shoes connected with the ground, and she thought, *Yes, I do feel grounded and connected to the Earth*, and this feeling was comforting and reassuring. She felt anchored and safe, but around her she could visualise something like a shroud of mist, and she could sense that this was where another world, another dimension could exist, one which could not be seen, only sensed.

She slowly opened her eyes, still feeling that strong connection of her feet on the earth, and a single red rose in the vase before her came into her field of vision. She pressed her hand to her chest. As she tuned into the duality of her heartbeat and the rose, she knew what the mystery of the rose was. She may never be able to explain it to the Gardener, but she knew, deep down in her heart.

'Have you been making any progress?' the Gardener asked when he came in a little later, wiping his brow with the cloth he always had tucked in the back pocket of his trousers.

'I believe so,' Sophia said dreamily, 'I've started to join some dots.'

The Gardener nodded, knowing better than to ask.

It was just a very simple question.

'How are you feeling?' the Gardener had asked her, but it had stopped her in her tracks. She could not answer him.

She pursed her lips tight to stop a tsunami of words tumbling out.

'Did you see the new bench I have placed under the pergola of ramblers?' the Gardener asked before continuing quickly. 'Why don't you go and sit there for twenty minutes and contemplate my question, and then I'll ask you again how you are feeling.'

Sophia got up slowly and headed down to a part of the garden that was looking spectacular, and she loved walking through the tunnel of roses. Sitting on the bench, she forced herself to think about what the Gardener had asked her, and to examine her feelings. It was like opening a wardrobe she rarely looked in. Even the door was hard to open, so she just peered in through a small crack.

She had every reason to feel happy and contented, especially since she had found the garden, but she could feel an uncomfortable sensation in her chest as she realised that she carried all of her past sadness around with her. All of it, still hanging in the wardrobe. She did not want to revisit them, but it seemed she could not rid herself of them either.

Looking deeper, she saw that some of her saddest memories were intertwined with her happiest times, and so she held tight to all those sensations, afraid to let them go. Surrounded by roses on all sides, Sophia closed her eyes and began to breathe into the sadness that she felt, and slowly the heavy mass of pain began to soften and dissipate.

Sophia moved her head and neck, and gently rolled her shoulders, feeling the tension releasing. The heaviness in her chest was replaced by an orb of golden light. She could feel it spreading throughout her whole body, and continued to fill the space around her. She was soon surrounded by a golden aura of joyfulness and peace. And immersed in these new feelings, Sophia drifted back to the potting shed where the Gardener was waiting for her out on the verandah. He did not say a word, just held out his hands to her. She clasped them warmly and looked deeply into his eyes.

'Thank you,' she said. 'Thank you so much.'

'You are welcome, Sophia. Very welcome,' he replied.

As soon as Sophia walked in the door of the potting shed on a fresh Autumn morning, she knew that the Gardener had discovered something. There was a frisson of expectation in the air, but it was mainly his face that gave it away.

The Gardener was not a young man; his face showed the years spent in the baking sun, the days in the wind trying to tie back rose canes to prevent them breaking, and the hours out in the frost wrapping the young plants in hessian to protect them from the onslaught of Winter.

But today his face had a luminous glow, his eyes sparkled, and his skin had a smoothness and relaxed quality. Whatever he had come across had erased the tension and fatigue of many years of hard work and worry. For a moment Sophia did not speak, not wanting to break the spell whilst she bathed in the glorious anticipation of what was to be revealed.

From behind his back the Gardener pulled out some coloured brochures for the Kashan Rosewater Festival.

'Listen to this,' he said excitedly. 'Ancient cities in the Iranian desert, the sound of flowing water, the song of the nightingale, and the fragrance of thousands of roses fill the air. Can you just imagine it? Surrounding mountains protect the rose gardens from the heat of the desert. And each rose bloom being picked by hand in the early morning.' The Gardener's eyes were closed as he described it all to Sophia.

'I would like to go to the festival this year,' he said, eyes open now and looking at Sophia almost beseechingly, 'and I'm not getting any younger. And you never know, I might find the answer to our mystery.'

Sophia thought he should go, too; she would love to hear all about it, and she had never seen him look so animated. Well, apart from the times when new water shoots sprouted, or when a new rose bloomed for the first time. So, with her blessing, she had waved the Gardener goodbye as he set off for the Rosewater Festival. He looked like a young boy with his tiny suitcase and a spring in his step. He had left her with a list of jobs to do and a feeling of disquietude in her heart.

The sound of running water filled the courtyard, and diamonds of sparkling light danced on the central pond. The air was rich with the fragrance of damask roses. At a small mosaic table in the corner two elderly men sipped mint tea from fancy gold etched glasses.

'It's been a long time,' the bearded man in the striped robe said to the smooth-shaven Westerner in the floppy gardener's hat. 'What brings you here, my friend?'

The second man flipped the latches on his small brown case and pulled out a pile of papers. A flicker of recognition and a smirk crossed the face of the hirsute man.

'Still you can't see it, can you? How many years have you been trying? Let us take a walk.'

The two men strolled out into the main enclosed garden, startling a white peacock dozing in the shade.

'You know we call these gardens "paridaiza", meaning "a walled garden". The garden, a piece of paradise on earth, yes? Yes, you can understand that, but the rose itself is much more than that. The rose, intrigue, timelessness, devotion, wisdom, beauty, love, and balance.'

The two men walked, and talked, and talked some more as the light began to fade and the desert sun dipped behind the sand dunes and illuminated the sky in vibrant orange and dusty pink.

The stars were bright and clear out in the desert, pinned on a dark navy velvet backdrop. Farid and the Gardener had talked well into the night, perhaps not solving all the world's problems, but knowing what was at the root of them. The topic drifted back often to the rose, the language they both understood.

Farid cleared his throat and began to speak, his voice clear and strong travelling out into the night.

'I don't know when we will meet again my friend. What I am about to say, you already know, but I want to spell it out. The rose complements and completes us, relaxes and restores us. It connects us with our true selves, and enables us to see what we need to see; it speaks to all of our senses, is tied to our memories. It adds richness to our lives, and another dimension. The Ancient Egyptians and Romans believed that the rose would ease the passage between this world and the next, but the rose holds no sway with time, sees no separation between the worlds. The rose speaks of wholeness, a never-ending cycle, no beginnings or endings, no grief or loss; only renewal, peace, and profound joy. The mystery of the rose cannot be put into words, only felt deep in your heart. The rose awakens the concept of paradise within us, and once you can feel it you are never lost, or lonely, or discontented. You have an infinite source of energy and inner resilience to draw on, no matter what is going on around you; you can retreat to this inner point of stillness and from your innate wisdom and strength respond accordingly.'

Simultaneously the two men held their hands to their chests, bowed gently to each other, and went their separate ways.

Even though the Gardener was still away she continued their routine just with a smaller pot of tea.

When she lifted the tea caddy the lightness of it reminded her that she had used the last of the tea the day before. Not realising how much she now enjoyed this moment of not really doing anything except contemplating the day ahead, she pulled the bentwood chair over to the dresser and jumped up to have a look on the top shelf where she knew the Gardener kept his stash of tea, and what he called his 'special treats'. There were several small hexagonal boxes of Turkish Delight, a tin of French rose and lemon-flavoured boiled sweets, and she was pleased to find a fresh box of tea right at the very back of the cupboard. The Gardener had enjoyed opening a packet of tea and getting her to smell the fragrance.

'Remember this smell. Some say this is what the tea roses, the roses I was showing you in the heritage border, were named after; others say it was because the roses came across the seas from exotic lands on the tea clippers. They were originally called Tea Scented China Roses.'

Sophia looked forward to inhaling the aroma of the tea and reinforcing her memory for the fragrances associated with roses, but as she picked up the box of tea she saw quite clearly the brown paper parcel tied up with string, with her name on a square of paper on the front. To see her name in the cupboard was a surprise, but nothing seemed to shock her anymore. The writing was in the Gardener's hand, and he obviously meant her to find the package when she was in the mood for a cup of tea or rifling his cupboard for a sweet treat.

Did that say anything about the meaning of the parcel? Was it something that would bring refreshment, or was it an indulgence, an extravagance, or a delicacy? When she read the note on the parcel, the task seemed very decadent.

Don't open the package until you have collected one of each of the following blooms: Papa Meilland, Mr Lincoln, Crimson Glory, Fragrant Cloud, and Munstead Wood. Take a cushion and the package and the roses to the sunny corner of the courtyard, then open the package and enjoy.

Glancing down the list of roses, she knew most of them; they were red, fragrant, and intense. Without a moment's hesitation, Sophia gathered what she needed and began the task. At this time of year, it was not hard to find these red roses, and Sophia marvelled at all the different reds in her basket and the perfume of the blended aromas. Not wanting the stunning array of blooms to wilt, she slipped them in her water bottle and made herself comfortable on the garden bench. Gently pulling off each piece of tape without tearing the paper, Sophia opened the package to reveal a beautiful brocade-covered box with a hinged lid and a brass clasp. As she released the clasp, the lid sprung open and inside was what looked to be a tangle of silk ribbons of assorted muted colours. On each ribbon, delicately embroidered, were quotes by Hafiz and Rumi. The Gardener had mentioned the two Persian poets to Sophia recently, and she was intrigued to see what quotes he had selected especially for her.

From Hafiz:

Stay close to anything that makes you glad you are alive.

I wish I could show you, when you are lonely or in darkness, the astonishing light of your own being.

The words you speak become the house you live in.

And from Rumi:

**Every sweet-scented rose tells from its heart the secrets
of heaven and earth.
Where there is rain there is hope for treasure.
The rose's rarest essence lives in the thorn.
The rose celebrates by falling apart.
It's time to speak of roses and pomegranates, and of
the oceans where pearls are made.
If your thought is a rose, you are a rose garden.
Let the beauty of what you love be what you do.
Everyone sees the unseen in proportion to the clarity
of their heart.
What you seek is seeking you.**

Sophia was smiling and thinking what a special man the Gardener was. She had never had a wiser or more thoughtful friend. Looking at the quotes, she started to put them in order of how much they seemed to be speaking to her, and little by little she began to see herself in a whole new light. She felt she could see the stepping stones to creating a more joyful life.

The rain was pouring down; what had started as a gentle shower had now built up to such an intensity that the gutters on the potting shed were not up to the job and curtains of water cascaded down in front of the windows. It was the type of rain that does not happen very often, but it makes you sit up and take notice, and be thankful that you are inside.

It was a Saturday, and Sophia had been looking forward to spending time out amongst the roses. She was at her happiest when she could wander from bloom to bloom, even if she did question whether it was right to talk to the roses …

But the rain was showing no signs of easing up; she would not be going out there today. The paths were muddy rivulets, and on some of the rose beds she could see the mulch rising up and drifting away.

Disappointed about her change of plans, and feeling restless at being trapped in for the afternoon, with a heavy sigh and heavier eyelids Sophia dropped onto her favourite seat and sank into the plump cushions. At that moment she surrendered to all of the shoulds, musts, and coulds that were always running rampant through her head, and she just let go and gave in fully to the sensation that there was nowhere she needed to go, and nothing she needed to do. She lightly closed her eyes and, although she could still hear the rain outside and smell the damp earth, in her mind's eye she could see the rose garden on a warm Spring afternoon. Feeling totally safe, contented and calm, Sophia found she could stroll through the garden, inspect the roses, and see their vivid beauty. It was as if the rose garden was now within her, and she could return to and enter the garden whenever she needed to. Tuning in to the sound of the rain streaming and gurgling, she could feel it washing away all her worries and cares, and the sadness and grief that had clung to her and refused to budge.

The deluge outside had the power and intensity to wash and scour everything clean, and Sophia began to feel an incredible lightness in her being.

A powder-pink envelope was pinned to the door of the potting shed with a cluster of miniature pink Cecile Brunner rosebuds when Sophia arrived the next morning. There was no name on the envelope, but she knew it was meant for her.

She put the letter in the middle of the antique writing desk and placed on top of it the millefiori (a thousand flowers) Venetian glass paperweight. With the note secure, she stepped to the back of the shed and filled a small fluted vase with water, arranged the cluster of rosebuds in it, and carried them back to the desk. Sitting down, she observed that her hands were shaking and, feeling that the contents of the pink envelope were going to be earth-shattering, she realised that the anticipation of the possibilities for her was so delectable that she didn't want the moment to pass. So, she did the only sensible thing and got up, locked the door, and made herself a cup of tea.

Her cup rattling in the saucer, she sat down again with a deep sigh. She focused on her breathing for a few minutes, and took a few sips of her tea that was far too hot. She put the cup and saucer to one side and reached for the letter opener. The handle of the letter opener was quite stunning, with a plethora of repousse scroll work and a pierced lattice end surrounded by floral motifs. The symbols on the blade showed it was sterling silver and it was pleasingly heavy in her hand.

She picked up the paperweight for a moment, looking at the pink swirls of glass, and felt as if she was being drawn down into the vortex inside the glass dome. She put it down with a small thud; the sound was like a knock on the door of her consciousness and she picked up the letter. There was nothing flimsy about the paper of the envelope; it had a fine grain of cold-pressed handmade watercolour paper, and was delightful to touch. She ran her fingers along the deckle edges, the sensation sending tingles up her arm. She raised the envelope to her nose and inhaled the rich rose scent. Not the scent of a cheap perfume, no; this heady aroma was the real thing – it was *attar of roses*. That fragrance told her more than the contents of the letter could, and even if the letter was blank inside, she knew that the Gardener had gone straight to the source of the mystery. She knew that the Gardener had communed with Farid Uddin Attar.

Finally, Sophia slit the envelope open and extricated the note inside. The paper folded in half had a small diagram of geometric shapes and written very simply in the same feathery font:

When we enter the garden,
the garden enters us.

Sophia examined the diagram, finding it somewhat familiar. Looking around, her eyes landed on a Persian rug at her feet with the same rectangular shapes.

'Oh, a garden plan. A Persian garden!' Sophia laughed out loud, excited to be discovering answers to the clue. From the bookcase she pulled down one of the dusty tomes, *Persian Gardens: Their Symbology and Meaning*. Sophia began to search for more answers. A fragile frayed red ribbon revealed a page where one paragraph had been underlined faintly in pencil.

'Gardens are a symbol of a sanctuary in the desert offering rest and respite from the harsh world outside, an example of the beauty that could be created in an unfriendly world.'

She sat with that thought for a moment, her eyes closed, her elbows on the desk, and her face resting in the palms of her hands. As she contemplated the thought, she found her breathing was becoming slower and deeper, and she was filled with a sense of calm.

Opening her eyes and bringing the words on the note into focus, Sophia suddenly understood what it meant. She could feel the same sense of peace deep within her that she only thought she could experience when she was in the garden amongst the roses.

The shadows of the rose bushes were long as they stretched out on that lazy Autumn afternoon. There was not a cloud in the sky, just a faint haze from the smoke of someone, somewhere close, burning off. The last rays of the sun gave off little heat as Sophia sat on the bench, but she lifted her face skywards and just felt the rosy glow of the sun through her closed eyelids.

She thought the Gardener would have returned by now. He had spoken of leaving the last flush of blooms on the bushes just before the cool days of Winter extended their chilly fingers into those bright Autumn days. Now was the time when the bushes were given permission to set their hips; plump, vibrant berries, a food source for birds over Winter.

The Gardener had explained how the rose hips were harvested in monastery gardens and made into syrups and medicines rich in Vitamin C, and of course, the rose hips were the source of the seed. Depending on which blooms the bees had visited, there was always the chance that a special hybrid had been created – 'A source of wonder,' he had exclaimed. Growing roses from seed was notoriously difficult, but sometimes a bush would self-seed, leaving a little surprise and not revealing all its secrets until the rose bloomed.

So deep in thought on the cycles of the season, Sophia was not aware of someone approaching until she heard the crunch of the gravel as their footsteps halted right in front of her. Even then she was reluctant to open her eyes and pull herself back to the present moment and the inevitable busyness and activity that would ensue if she acknowledged that she was 'back'.

But inevitable it was, so she slowly inhaled and then, raising her eyelids that felt as heavy as lead, she saw before her the familiar silhouette, and the smile of the Gardener. He had returned.

At the furthest end of the garden was a wild rose that had grown into a thicket. It made the perfect fence; there was no way you could get through it without being torn to shreds. It was incredibly dense, with branches intertwining at all angles. When you stopped to look at it, it was quite entrancing. If you imagined it growing as if watching a time-lapse film reel, you could feel its vigour and the pulsating of life.

Sophia rarely came down this far as she felt there was something slightly wild and sinister about this part of the garden. But today she could not ignore it because a conglomerate of bird species had descended on the ripe red rose hips. The chirping and excited activity was mesmerising, and she wanted to observe the phenomenon.

At that moment, the Gardener appeared with his basket. 'It happens like this every year,' he explained gleefully. 'The moment the rose hips are ripe, the birds come in and make so much noise about it that I grab my basket and join in the harvest. There is plenty for all to share, and this is part of the Autumn ritual that I love. There is something primal about making sure we are prepared for the coming Winter. And to feel in tune with Nature I continue this tradition, even though I know I can go to the supermarket at any minute.'

Now that was something Sophia could not imagine; the Gardener in the supermarket, foraging in the fruit and vegetable aisle. And he certainly seemed much more at home plucking the red jewels of the rose and quickly filling his basket whilst reciting recipes for fresh rose hip tea and a rose hip syrup.

Sophia woke up feeling dreadful. Her throat was scratchy and sore, her eyes were terribly tired, teary, and itchy, and her nose was hot and stuffy.

She struggled to untangle herself from the bedclothes and sat on the edge of the bed with her head in her hands and groaned. She knew she had a lot to do today, but how was she going to manage any of it feeling like this? She fumbled for her dressing gown and somehow made her way to the kitchen, the tiles cold on her bare feet. She opened the pantry, and peering in through her bleary eyes found a bottle of Vitamin C tablets with bioflavonoids. She turned the bottle over, and there was something to make her smile: *Rosa canina (Rosehips) extract equiv. to dry fruit 250mg*. She took one tablet with a few mouthfuls of icy water and then she remembered, *Oh, I can do even better than this!*

Locating her bag from the previous day somewhere between the front door and the lounge room, she felt a sense of hope when her hand clasped the little brown paper bag the Gardener had given her. Back in the kitchen she emptied the ruby red rosehips onto the stainless-steel benchtop and was delighted to see the warmth of Summer sun and the product of the bees' hard work glowing in her kitchen. Sophia found her ceramic tea-infusing cup; a mug with a little inner cup with holes in it and a close-fitting lid. Flicking the switch on the kettle, Sophia rinsed about one tablespoon of the hips under the tap. When the kettle clicked off, she poured the hot water over the glistening berries. Putting the lid on the mug to contain the volatile compounds, Sophia waited for ten minutes, filling in time seeking out a jar of honey that was not so crystallised that it needed to stand in hot water to avoid bending the spoon.

Lifting the lid and removing the porcelain strainer, Sophia was thrilled to see the rosy hue of the liquid. Stirring in a teaspoon of honey, Sophia smiled thinking of the bees and the roses reunited. Moving across to the window, she opened the curtain and saw a glimmer of the sun on the horizon. Closing her eyes to concentrate on sipping the health-giving liquid, Sophia felt her strength returning. When she opened her eyes, the sky was painted a warm apricot; it was going to be a good day after all.

The Gardener had several well-established trees in the garden through which he grew rambling roses.

'Rambling roses will grow up a tree quickly as they go in search of the light,' he explained to Sophia, 'but trees are solid and have tenacity. They grow slowly, but their growth is solid and reliable. Trees teach us to be patient. When we are impatient, we cannot see clearly; we are like the rambling roses heading blindly towards the light. The slow and steady growth of trees reminds us to pause before we react to situations, to step back and take a few breaths and live each moment of our lives without wishing away today or anticipating tomorrow.'

It had been a leisurely day in the garden. Sophia had wandered along the network of paths, removing a spent bloom here and a yellowing leaf there. The Gardener had disappeared early, murmuring something about a load of mulch, so Sophia had spent much of the day alone, except for the roses, and was blissfully happy.

Even though her chores had not been at all strenuous, she made her way to her favourite bench through the fragrant archway of blooms that were at their best right now. She had to look twice, because there was someone sitting on the bench peering kindly at her as she approached; an elderly lady with eyes of brightest blue and skin wrinkled with age, but looking so soft that Sophia had to resist stroking her cheek. Sophia was fascinated by older faces, believing you could tell a lot about a person's life by looking at the lines etched in their face. Here, Sophia could see a life with a lot of joy, some deep contemplation, and serene contentment.

'Ah, here you are,' the elderly lady said, her voice clear and warm as if she had been waiting for Sophia. Patting the bench beside her she added, 'Come sit down.' In her other hand she held a highly polished walking stick, beautifully carved with roses.

Sophia immediately felt comfortable in her presence and sat down eagerly. 'Do you live near here?' Sophia asked, keen to know more about this mysterious lady.

'Not far. I came on the bus,' she answered proudly.

'Do you come to the garden often?' Sophia enquired.

'Not so much these days, but I spent a lot of time here when I was younger. Let us just say I was a little bit lost after the death of my mother. I did not know where my life was heading or what I was meant to be doing, and one day I found myself in the garden. I was able to connect with my true self and made whole ...' her voice drifted off as she lost herself in distant and pleasant memories.

'Would you like a cup of tea?' Sophia finally asked after they had sat there together for a long time in deep and comfortable silence, as if they had known each other all their lives.

'That would be lovely,' she answered with a smile.

'Won't be a minute,' Sophia said, making a quick dash up to the shed, not wanting her unexpected guest to disappear before she returned. She was still there, real as day, when Sophia placed the tray on the bench between them.

A slightly shaky hand lifted the lid of the pot to inspect the brew. 'Ah, the rose petals and, of course, the Turkish Delight,' she laughed to herself as if enjoying a private joke. 'Let me pour.'

Sophia allowed herself be waited upon by this delightful creature; she was quite captivated by her. 'Do you live alone?' Sophia asked, curious to know more.

'No, not anymore, but I have my own quarters, and they are lovely. I am on the ground floor and I can step out through the French doors straight into the garden. I look out to a pergola, on one side of it is a climbing rose and on the other side is a grape vine. I love how the grape vine celebrates the seasons. It provides lovely shade in the heat of Summer, in Autumn it is a blaze of colour and I can collect all the Autumn shades of the leaves and take them inside and press them, in the Winter the bare vine lets the Winter sun in so I can sit behind the glass all cosy and warm, and when Spring comes it bursts into life with bright green leaves and the cycle continues on. And when the roses are in bloom and the grapes are on the vine I sit out in the courtyard and think of the days of wine and roses. I could sit out there all day on my own – it's blissful.'

Sophia could picture her sitting there, and she felt blissful, too. 'Do you have any family?' Sophia finally asked.

'Since spending time in this garden all those years ago, I felt my inner world become so rich that I was complete. I needed no one else, but that's not to say I didn't have wonderful people in my life. Most of them have gone on ahead of me, but I'm in no rush to move on, not when there are roses and the passing seasons to observe. But I must be getting back – I do not want to miss my dinner. I can have it in my room or up at the big house, wonderful food, fresh seasonal produce. You should see the vegetable patch and the orchard, just marvellous.'

And with a sprightliness that surprised Sophia, she was up and moving towards the side gate and the bus stop. Sophia accompanied her, not wanting the visit to be over.

'I so enjoyed our afternoon, it was lovely to spend time with you' she said as her bus pulled in.

Sophia helped her up the first step and said, 'But I never found out your name.'

'Oh, I thought you knew.' The stranger smiled gently, and just before the doors of the bus closed behind her, the elderly woman said warmly, 'I am Sophia.'

And the younger Sophia suddenly understood, and even though she was bewildered and disorientated, she knew without any doubt that everything in her life was going to be alright.

The moon was reflected in the ornamental pond surrounded by standard white Iceberg roses; the ripples made by the white swans swimming across the pond made it quiver as if it was winking.

Sophia stood in the shadows and watched this phenomenon, spellbound. She was so absorbed in the scene that she nearly jumped out of her skin when the gloved hand touched her lightly on the shoulder.

'Oh, I'm sorry to startle you, Sophia.' It was Michael.

'Oh no, that's alright,' Sophia said, already feeling more serene being in his presence. 'I was just caught up watching the swan playing with the moonbeams.'

Michael smiled warmly. 'The moonlit garden is full of magic. Come, let me show you,' he said, offering his hand which Sophia took without hesitation.

They moved quickly down the pathway. Sophia, being led, did not worry that she could not see where she was going, her feet barely touching the ground. The garden at night seemed a completely different place to the daytime garden, but Sophia was unconcerned as she was led further and further away from the potting shed. They arrived in a part of the garden that seemed very dark despite the moonlight.

'You might like to stop a moment here,' Michael said, and he was gone. Sophia stood there, her hand still outstretched from where he had been clasping it. She breathed in the night air deeply, and could pick up a slight spicy fragrance.

Mmm, cloves, she thought, and immediately she knew where she was in the garden. In her mind's eye she could see the velvety dark wine-purple ruffled petals and the bright yellow stamens of the vigorous climber with the unusual green-grey foliage. She spoke its name out into the darkness.

'Night Owl,' she breathed, and as if it was a command, silently the white barn owl with the heart-shaped face descended and landed on her outstretched hand. The sharp talons of the bird pressed into her flesh but did not pierce the skin. The bird's head swivelled so that it was looking straight at her and, illuminated by moonlight, the owl had an ethereal glow. Sophia held her breath and remained completely still, and she remembered that the Gardener had said something about an owl.

That's how he remembered my name, Sophia thought to herself. *The owl, a symbol of wisdom.* Her mind was ticking away, and she could feel things slipping into place.

'Wisdom,' she repeated to herself. 'Perhaps the owl knows the answer to the riddle, what the mystery hidden in the rose is. Who holds the mystery of the rose?' she whispered to the owl.

'Youuuuu,' the owl replied.

Winter

From the bottom of the garden Sophia could see small puffs of white smoke coming out of the red brick chimney tacked on the side of the potting shed.

Gathering all the garden implements into her wicker basket and wrapping her infinity scarf around her neck, Sophia surveyed the garden one more time. There was a stillness in the air, but also a sense of expectation. The clouds were a dark grey on the bottom but still light and fluffy on top. With no warning a light dusting of snow started to fall, accompanied by a sudden drop in temperature.

Sophia whirled around in wonder; she had never seen snow before. As she looked up to the sky, tiny snowflakes landed on her eyelashes and she laughed out loud despite the cold. The door of the potting shed suddenly swung open and Sophia gratefully swept inside to the warmth, and with her spare hand pulled the door shut behind her.

The garden was close to a busy road but the sounds of the cars could not be heard, the hedges forming a dense screen that not only hid the garden from view but also bounced the sound waves back from whence they came. The evergreen cypress hedges kept the garden quiet regardless of season, but in Winter without the birdsong it was at its most quiet.

Sophia had been fascinated as the Gardener told her about the different garden elements that contributed to the peacefulness: the rambling roses climbing up the potting shed wall; lawn instead of hard paved surfaces; and sources of white noise.

'White noise?' Sophia had asked, never having heard the term.

'Pleasant sounds that mask unwanted sounds,' the Gardener had explained. 'Think of the sound of water, an oasis in the desert. My favourite white noise in the garden is my bees buzzing.'

Sophia sat on the wooden bench rather than at her favourite spot on the wrought iron arbour seat, knowing that the wood would feel warmer on this cold grey day. It was as if she was viewing the garden in black and white, save for a scattering of red rose hips. The breeze was gentle, occasionally brushing her cheek lightly. The mood seemed to be sombre as the bare branches stood like sentries guarding the entry to another world, a world where roses always bloomed on bushes of rich green foliage. The branches might look barren and lifeless, but Sophia could feel beneath the surface the sap was moving, the life force and the soul of the roses had retreated within.

Just contemplating the slowing down of the roses' external activity made Sophia's heartrate and pulse slow, too. The cares and the frustrations of the world around her ceased to exist and, closing her eyes, she could feel things being reordered and rebuilt from within. The sensation of rejuvenation was intense, seeing herself becoming whole.

A stronger gust of wind made her open her eyes, just in time to see the sky dusted in pink as the sun slipped behind the clouds on the horizon. Feeling stronger and more powerful, Sophia left the garden with a sense of deep gratitude to the roses for sharing their wisdom.

Fog shrouded the garden like a thick blanket; the leafless branches of the roses were almost hidden. Sophia looked about her as she followed the familiar pathway to the potting shed. It was hard to believe it was the same place that had brought her so much joy throughout Spring and into Autumn. She was not sure why she had come to the garden today, as there would not be much to do.

The Gardener, detecting her despondency, met her in the doorway.

'Somewhere in the world there will always be roses blooming. You can seek them out, or seek them within. One day, Sophia, I hope you will see the everlasting roses that bloom in your heart and grow in the secret garden of your mind.' He spoke softly and gently, but with a firmness indicating that this was how it would be.

Sophia, not sure what he meant, but feeling a glimmer of hope and warmth starting to build in her chest.

'Please tell me more,' she asked, a little timidly.

'Do you have a favourite spot in the garden?' the Gardener began.

Sophia did a quick scan of the garden in her mind. That was a hard one; there were so many spots in the garden that she loved, but the seat at the end of the rose-covered arbour was the place she migrated to after a day of working hard at her gardening chores.

'Yes, the arbour seat,' she answered finally with a smile.

The Gardener smiled, too. 'When you close your eyes, can you see it clearly? Can you imagine the metal structure, the way the roses meet in the middle, and the dappled light on the ground? If you breathe in, can you smell the fragrance of the New Dawn and Compassion? Listen – can you hear the bees buzzing, and feel the gentle breeze on your face?' he asked.

'Yes, yes I can,' Sophia said enthusiastically, as she engaged her senses and was transported to the Summer garden.

'Good, good,' the Gardener encouraged. 'Practice this often and you will find the scene becomes more and more real until it exists in your mind and heart as much as it does in the garden.'

Sophia's footsteps made a delightful crunching sound as she walked across the frosted lawn. Frosts were a rare occurrence here, making the novelty of them seem even more magical. The garden was coated in white as if some fairy chef had been busy overnight covering everything with a sugar frosting, including a few last blooms on the roses.

The garden seemed especially still today, not even a trill of a bird or a breath of wind. The clouds cleared from the sky and the weak Winter sunlight glistened on the frost-encrusted plants and started the thaw, water droplets making their slow descent to the soil.

Rugged up against the cold, Sophia enjoyed watching the colour return to the garden as the frost dissipated and, in her mind she kept wondering, *Will this be the last frost of Winter? Will the garden wake again coated in white, or have the cogs moved on and we are on the way to Spring?*

Sophia could not think straight. There was a feeling that something had to happen, a major shift in her world. She could feel the intense pent-up sensation in her chest. She felt she was on the cusp of something, but without the accompanying excitement; there was a dread that nothing would change, and a fear that something would and that she would not be able to cope. How did she ever wind up in this situation? She could feel the deep lines of a frown on her forehead, and even when she relaxed her face she could still feel the ridges there.

She took a seat in the walled garden; at least she was protected from the winds here. Closing her eyes, she tuned into the sounds of the garden. The garden felt very empty without the bees buzzing, a lonely blackbird scratched around in the mulch, and Sophia was surprised to hear the whirr of a dove's wings as it took flight. But nothing else stirred.

Here she was trapped in limbo, frozen in time, as if she had slipped through into another layer of existence, submerged but still breathing. The only thing that felt real now was the heaviness in her heart, acting like a lead weight holding her down, but giving her a focus, or even a purpose, to conquer this feeling and rise above it. She concentrated on her breathing, and slowly she could feel her chest expanding like a balloon inflating, and with each inhalation she began to feel lighter and less burdened. The sensation was so enthralling that she felt as if she could float into the air. She kicked off her gardening clogs as if they were the weight that was holding her down, and soon she could feel herself rising higher and higher above the garden.

Looking down, she could see the layout of the garden, the curved pathways forming the shape of a five-petal rose. She felt no fear or wonder; she just felt free, and thought, *This is how I am meant to feel.* And then she rested, feeling supported and at ease.

The sound of slow footsteps and the tinkle of a china teacup eventually woke her.

'I thought you might like a cup of tea,' the Gardener said, putting down a tray and handing Sophia a crocheted rug he had folded over his arm. 'It is getting a bit chilly out here.'

'I hadn't noticed,' Sophia said, putting her shoes back on and gladly wrapping herself in the rug.

The Gardener just smiled that sweet, knowing smile.

The Gardener was hard at work at his potting table when Sophia popped her head in the door on a clear Winter's day. His pruning tools were all laid out on a towel in front of him and he was cleaning the blades of his secateurs, loppers, and a small pruning saw with steel wool and soapy water. Sophia could see the metal becoming shiny, not a hint of black, looking brand new.

He dried each tool carefully. Taking his well-loved red-handled secateurs in his hand, he said to Sophia, 'Take a careful look at these. There are two blades, but this is the cutting blade and the one that we sharpen. Look at the cutting blade, it has two sides – a flat side and an angled side. With your diamond sharpening stone, keeping it flat on the flat side of the blade and just rub the stone in a circular motion to remove any burrs or pits. Then turn the secateurs over and, matching the angle of the blade with the stone, work your way along sharpening the angled edge. Now these will give you a good, clean, sharp cut that will make sure you are not damaging the rose bushes. A clean cut heals quickly and prevents disease entry.'

Sophia noticed that the Gardener had cleaned two sets of the tools and had two pairs of gauntlet gloves laid out. Putting one set of tools and a kneeling pad and gloves into a basket, he handed it to her saying, 'Here's your pruning kit. Let the fun begin.'

Sophia had enjoyed doing the light prune at the end of Summer, but the Winter pruning was the real pruning, the Gardener had told her. And the Gardener's excitement was catching. She could not wait for the lesson to begin.

'Gosh, I love doing the Winter pruning,' the Gardener said as they walked to the far end of the garden. 'It is the most satisfying job of the year. Not only are you tidying up each plant, but you are creating the future growth patterns and stimulating the plant into action. And the best part is you get to spend time with every rose bush, working out its needs and wants and dreaming of its future. By pruning in late Winter ...'

'After the last frost,' they chorused together.

'… the plants have taken back the nutrients they can reuse, so most of the leaves will have dropped,' the Gardener continued. 'This allows you to see what you are doing. First thing is to cut out any dead or diseased branches. The bushes will look better immediately, and you are making room for new growth. Also remove any branches that are rubbing or crossing over each other. Once again you are creating space and opening up the centre of the bush for better air flow and less disease. And then you are looking to remove about two-thirds of the height cutting just above an outward facing bud.'

The Gardener showed Sophia what the bud eyes looked like, and she could see that some of the bushes were starting to sprout with their new growth already. Sophia loved how the roses were giving her direction on where to make the cuts. Working alongside the Gardener, Sophia picked up the pruning techniques and before long she was smiling as widely as the Gardener as they worked out the puzzle of each of the bushes. After finishing each rose bush Sophia and the Gardener surveyed their work, going back in to neaten up a cut or take a bit more off here and there. It was surprising how quickly they made progress, and when the light started to fade that afternoon they were halfway back to the potting shed.

'So, Sophia,' the Gardener said, straightening out the cricks in his back, 'how did you enjoy your first day of serious pruning?'

Sophia thought for a moment, even though she knew the answer. She could not remember a more satisfying day in her life. 'I loved it,' she finally said, 'I really did, it was if each bush was talking to me.'

The Gardener was beaming, 'I knew you would enjoy it and I think you will sleep well tonight.'

The Gardener was right there; Sophia slept like a log, a deep and satisfying sleep, and woke up feeling bright and refreshed and ready to tackle the day's pruning.

Rose petals were scattered on the floor of the potting shed, but the Gardener himself was nowhere to be seen. There were no dishes on the sink, the fireplace was swept clean. Even the potting table that usually had some spilled soil, a tumble of pots, a small trowel, and maybe some gardening gloves, was spotless. There was no sign of life. The cushions were plumped, and the throw rugs were unwrinkled, their diagonal points centred perfectly.

Sophia pulled on the cord to turn on the lamp, not so much to counter the impending darkness, but to drive out the feeling of desolation and emptiness. She admitted gravely to herself that she knew absolutely nothing about the Gardener; he had never told her anything much about himself, where he lived, if he had family other than his son. She was horrified with herself; she did not even know his name.

He had always been here whenever she arrived in the morning and would walk with her to the door whenever she left to go home. Until this very moment she had never been curious; she just took for granted his constant presence and simple ways. The shed, which had always felt so welcoming and fascinating, now felt old and dusty and decaying. The rose petals on the floor struck her as odd, with everything else seeming so in order. Why were the petals there, and where were the stems and leaves?

The bin under the writing table appeared empty, but she lifted it up and moved toward the light to make sure, and in doing so noticed the envelope that was propped up by a bottle of ink. With trembling hands Sophia flipped over the envelope, which had been sealed with a red wax seal bearing the imprint of a rose. She did not want to open it for two reasons: she was fearful of what the envelope would contain, and what impact it would have on her future. The solace of the garden and the companionship and wisdom of the Gardener had become the balm that soothed her jangled nerves, that gave her a reason to get up in the morning, and that made her life a meaningful existence and a real source of joy. If this was all to come to an end now, she didn't know what she would do. And the sealing wax summed up everything that made the garden and its gardener special. It was from another era; sealing wax was commonly in use around the 16th century, around the time of Attar. It was a mystery, it was an embellishment on what could be a mundane item, it was a thing of beauty, it symbolised privacy and indicated that the letter would not have been seen by anyone else but her. The thought of breaking the seal was unbearable, so she took out the letter opener and slit the top of the envelope open.

Three words were written on the card in the Gardener's familiar calligraphic flourish:

Nuper Rosarum Flores

Feeling mystified, she reached for Richard Bird's *A Gardener's Latin: The Language of Plants Explained* but was left none the wiser. Sophia was reluctant to use the internet to find the answer as the Gardener believed that books and contemplation held the answers to most questions. So instead of reaching for her phone, Sophia flicked on the radio that never moved from the Gardener's favourite station, ABC Classic. As the richly-textured music with angelic voices filled the potting shed, Sophia, feeling comforted, closed her eyes and really listened to the music. The first thing that came to her was that she could not understand a word of what was being sung, but the sounds of the words and the melody were lifting her spirits. She could feel her breathing becoming slower and more regular as she began to relax. By the time the piece had finished and the announcer began to speak, her mood had altered considerably.

No longer fearful, she was excited by the challenge the Gardener had presented her with. What had made her turn on the radio? Was she just trying to fill in the emptiness with something?' She thought again about the words the Gardener had left for her and yes, she knew they were Latin and the music she had just listened to was in Latin, too.

Sophia went to the Gardener's record collection and it was not long before she found what she was looking for. *Nuper Rosarum Flores*, composed in 1436 to mark the occasion of the completion of the Duomo di Firenze, the dome in the cathedral in Florence, formerly the Cattedrale di Santa Maria del Fiore, the Cathedral of Saint Mary of the Flower. The composition speaks of how there were garlands of yellow roses in the cathedral despite a difficult winter.

Gathering up a handful of the yellow petals from the floor and slipping them into the envelope with the card and depositing it safely into her handbag, she decided it was time to lock up and head home.

Harold at the front desk unlocked the glass door to the apartment building when she buzzed the intercom. She was not usually back this late.

'In for the night now?' he asked.

Sophia nodded, unable to speak, realising why the garden was so important to her. This place where she lived four floors up, with no garden, no balcony, and with someone always watching your coming and going felt like a prison of sorts. She always caught the lift to her floor, even though it would probably be quicker and good exercise for her to go up the stairs, but she hated the feeling of being in the stairs with the fire doors that only opened one way. So, she watched the orange numbers slowly descending and finally the doors opened. She stepped inside. A strong smell of takeaway food filled the lift, and she wondered if it was possible for this place she called home to be less homely or welcoming. She could not go on living like this, it was unbearable.

Sophia was reminded of something the Gardener had told her.

'Roses will come into their full glory only if they are planted in a situation that meets their needs. If planted in the wrong place, even the healthiest and most robust rose will become sickly and not flower properly.'

Despair started to weigh down on her like a wet blanket, but the ping of the door jolted her memory; the envelope. Perhaps that would give her a clue to what she must do.

She began to heat up her evening meal, a soup she had made, rich with lentils and root vegetables and fragrant with herbs. She may have to sleep metres above the ground, but this meal always connected her to the earth, a garden in a bowl. As she enjoyed her soup with slices of crusty sourdough rye bread, her mind went back to a conversation she and the Gardener had had about appreciating the seasons. In air-conditioned cubicles, cut off from the outside world you could wear the same thing every day and never notice the difference. Tuning in to the seasons is the only way to truly experience life, to be alive, to feel a scorching northerly wind from across the desert or the chill in the breeze swept down over snow-capped mountains. To be caught in a sudden downpour of tropical splendour, and watch the earth parched by a hot summer taking up the rain hungrily and gratefully. To be part of the great cycle of life that is going on around us. To see the leaves change to a fiery mass of colour before letting go and leaving the branches bare; to see blossoms and then bright green leaves burst forth from a lifeless structure.

The following morning, Sophia was still excited by what she had researched the night before about the clue referring to Florence, and she had a read about the rose garden from which you could look back to the city and see the Duomo. Florence was somewhere she had always wanted to visit. Every time she walked pass the Il Papiro shop in the laneway she would go in, and it always felt like she was stepping into a shop in another country. She loved looking at the high-quality stationery and the wax seals and she knew that the message on this beautiful handcrafted paper would have to be something of significance. You wouldn't get out your fountain pen and textured paper and write your shopping list; in fact, Sophia found it hard to imagine that in her life she would ever have the occasion to use such stationery. Who would she send it to, for a start? Sophia made herself stop imagining there as the familiar pain clenched her heart and a tear ran quickly down her cheek.

Then she gave into it. There was one person above all who she would love to send such a letter to, but there is no forwarding address to there, wherever *there* is or whatever it is. Still, she could still write the letter and post it. There would be no harm in that. All the better if it was posted in Florence with an Italian stamp and postmark.

'Yes,' she said out loud, and decided then and there to go. She would write to her mother who would have loved to read such a letter, or who better still would have loved to accompany her there and enjoy the adventure in a way only mothers and daughters could. So she grabbed her keys and her bag and headed for the door. She would make her first stop the travel agent, and then drop by the office to put in her application for annual leave.

The travel agency was busy, with each of the seats in front of the agents taken. This did not worry Sophia because it gave her a chance to think of what she would say when it was her turn. A wall of coloured brochures assaulted her senses with images of tall buildings, bridges, opera houses, and someone holding up a starfish whilst wearing a mask and snorkel on their head. This was all a far cry away from the handmade Florentine card and envelope with the red wax seal.

Perhaps what she was going to do was all wrong; since when had she been so impulsive and unpredictable? Well, that would have to be since she discovered the rose garden. Just picturing the winding pathways scattered with petals and the lush green foliage, Sophia could feel her panic subsiding, feel herself becoming calmer and more rational. And no, she did not head for the door; she stepped up to the desk when she heard a bright voice say, 'Next please.'

Taking a seat, Sophia was comforted to hear her request sound so reasonable and sensible, almost every day.

'Florence would be beautiful at this time of year, lucky you, and you'll never guess what arrived this morning,' the travel agent gushed. 'This is where I'd love to stay the next time I go to Florence.'

On the glossy brochure clasped in her hand Sophia read, *Belmond Villa San Michele is the nearest thing to heaven to be found on this earth.*

'It used to be an old monastery, now it's a beautiful hotel up in the hills overlooking the city. They'll pick you up from the airport.'

Sophia took one glance at the front of the brochure and, seeing the manicured gardens and green lawns, urns of cascading roses, the cypress trees, and the view down to the ancient city, said diffidently, 'That would be wonderful, thank you, but I think it is a bit out of my league.'

'Hmm,' the travel agent sighed. 'Wait, wait.' She went through some papers in her desk draw. 'Ah, here it is,' she said, pulling out a cream card embossed with the Lily Iris Florentia, the ancient symbol of Florence. 'One of my clients stays here in Florence, I think it might be up near the rose garden you want to visit. It's just a few rooms run by two sisters, clean and comfortable, I believe. You can have this, I'll look up the address,' she said, sliding the card across to Sophia.

Sophia's eyes widened when she saw the name of one of the sisters was Rosa. That was just the sign Sophia was looking for.

'This sounds just what I need. Could you please book me a week's accommodation with flights?'

The seatbelt sign pinged off and the cabin erupted with movement. Sophia took the fine stationery compendium from her seat pocket and lowered her tray table. She arranged a piece of paper neatly and opened her fountain pen with a satisfying click.

Where to begin, she thought. Is there anything more heartbreaking than knowing you can never speak with someone ever again? Oh, certainly you can talk to them, you can have conversations over and over in your head with them, one-sided conversations, conversations they might not hear or sense – or maybe they can – but you will never know, and they will never respond.

So were the thoughts pestering Sophia as she cruised at 30,000 feet on her way to Florence, her pen poised and her page blank. Why did she feel that she must write this letter that would never be received and never be read? What folly was this?

But then the words began to flow; what started as a trickle soon became a torrent, and she wrote on and on through tear-clouded eyes, the person next to her tearing their eyes away from the tiny screen in front of them when the occasional sob escaped Sophia's lips. She wrote of sadness, loneliness, and regret, of missed opportunities, and moments unshared. But she also wrote about the rose garden and the Gardener. And when she had finished writing and sealed the envelope, she closed her red-rimmed eyes and slipped into a deep and dreamless sleep.

Sophia was relieved that Florence Airport was small and welcoming, with only one runway and a short ride on the Tramvia to the centre of the city. The two sisters who ran the guesthouse welcomed her warmly with espresso coffee in tiny gold-rimmed cups and homemade almond biscotti.

Her room was on the top floor of the building looking out onto the river. Sophia bought a postage stamp from the reception desk and walked out onto the cobblestone streets to find a red postbox. Not knowing a word of Italian, she chose the slot which read *PER TUTTE LE ALTRE DESTINAZION* and posted her weighty letter, feeling a weight lift from her heart. She continued to walk along the river until she came to a small café where she sat at a tiny table under a striped awning and let the flow of the river wash her cares away.

Sophia woke the next morning to golden sunlight streaming across the floor of the room, the lace curtain dancing playfully in the breeze. She jumped from her bed feeling a sense of excitement and anticipation for this was the day she was to visit the Giardino delle Rose, her reason for making this rather impulsive trip.

She was the first guest to come down to breakfast and was glad of the solitude to get her thoughts in order as she sat out on the terrace near the cumquat trees and glazed pots of herbs. She drew herself a simple map. It was not far to walk, but navigation wasn't one of her strong points and she didn't want to have to ask anyone for directions. The day promised to be warm, so with her hat, sunglasses, walking shoes, and a small thermos flask of tea – she had smiled to herself, thinking of the Gardener as she had slipped that into her backpack – she made tracks heading out along the Lungarno Serristori. She was quickly past the wild open space of Terzo Giardino with its geometric paths mown through tall grasses, and a sandy beach area with deck chairs. She turned right when she saw the Tower of San Niccolò and began to climb gently above the city to the Viale Giuseppe Poggi, named after the Florentine architect who created the rose garden in 1865.

Even though Sophia had seen photos of the garden, she still felt her heart leap when she saw the rose bushes come into view. Wandering along the stone paths she kept turning around to look back down over the city of Florence to see the views of the terracotta tiled roofs and the majestic Duomo of the Florence Cathedral that this garden was famous for. Every scene of the city was framed in roses, and Sophia marvelled at the beauty of it.

When she came to the top of the garden, Sophia could see two women sitting on a park bench looking out at the view. Even from quite a distance away Sophia knew that they were a mother and daughter, and in her heart she felt the familiar pang of grief. Sophia did not want to disturb their moment of peace; they, too, had arrived at the garden early to enjoy the serenity and avoid the crowds. But all the same, she was drawn to them and longed to hear what they were talking about so intently.

As Sophia moved closer ever so slowly, she could not believe her eyes at how similar the two women looked to her own mother and grandmother. Sophia kept putting one foot in front of the other towards them almost robotically, as if in a dream. When finally she could hear their voices she stopped abruptly, unable to move any further. She could do nothing but stop and stare because there in front of her, there was no mistaking, was her mother speaking to *her* own mother.

Sophia was rendered motionless like one of the bronze sculptures in the garden. The two ladies were reading and discussing a letter, passing pages to each other. And it wasn't just any letter – it was the letter Sophia had sobbed over as she wrote it on the plane, the same letter she had posted on her arrival in the city.

'So much pain, so much anguish. It breaks my heart to read this,' Sophia's mother said. 'Sophia is drowning in her grief, it is so sad. I wish we could help her. Does she have to say goodbye to us? To leave us behind to move on happily with her life?'

Sophia's grandmother shook her head and then said in a clear, considered voice, sounding much younger and more vibrant than Sophia remembered her, 'I am sure she doesn't want to let go of those sad feelings because then she would have to let go of us and be truly alone. She is bound to us with her sadness, and knowing how stubborn she is, she will never let us go.'

'I wish we could let her know that we are happy and contented, and that she doesn't have to let go of us, just the sad feelings she has when she thinks of us,' Sophia's mother continued. 'If only we could let her know to remember us with love, think of us smiling warmly at her, and let that feeling fill her heart; for in a heart full of love, there is no room for sadness.'

'I have a feeling Sophia now knows that we are always with her, she has surely felt our presence whenever she is in the rose garden.'

Sophia could see her mother and grandmother folding up the letter and preparing to go. She longed to call out and run to them, but not a sound would come out of her mouth and her legs felt as though they were made of marble.

And then suddenly the bells of the Cathedral of Florence rang out, making Sophia jump, and finally she found she could move, turning to look in the direction of where the sound was coming from. Swivelling quickly back to the park bench, she opened her mouth wide to yell out to her mother, but the sound she uttered was more like a whimper when she saw that the bench was empty except for a crumpled envelope. Once again she was left alone.

Sophia collapsed onto the seat and cradled her head in her hands as she tried to remember the words her mother and grandmother had said. Gradually feeling calmer, Sophia started to smile, and she took out her cup and thermos flask and poured herself a cup of tea. Sipping her tea, and looking out over the city of Florence, she thought of her mother and her grandmother, and she thought of the Gardener, too. A warmth filled her chest and her whole being as her mother's words returned to her.

'In a heart full of love there is no room for sadness.'

When Sophia's plane touched down in the early hours of the morning it was cold and grey, but the day was fine. As the glass double doors slid open, Sophia knew there would be no one there to meet her so she headed straight to the airport bus. Because she was travelling light, Sophia thought that there was no need to head straight home and so continued past her bus stop to the garden.

The Gardener greeted her out the front of the potting shed as if he had been expecting her. 'Excellent timing, Sophia. I have just put the kettle on. I am glad your trip was a success. Thank you for the postcard.'

'The postcard?' Sophia queried, suddenly feeling ashamed that she had not thought to send him one.

'Yes, it arrived yesterday,' he said holding out a postcard with a beautiful view of the Florence skyline framed by rose bushes in full bloom. Sophia knew exactly where the photo had been taken. She turned the card over surreptitiously to see what was written on the back.

For a start, there was no name or address on it. The writing that looked suspiciously like her own simply said, *'Do not watch the petals fall from the rose with sadness, know that, like life, things sometimes fade, before they can bloom again ~ Rumi.'*

'The catalogues have arrived!' the Gardener said cheerfully, fanning out a selection of colourful brochures from rose nurseries on the table in front of Sophia.

She picked up the first one and flicked through it. The names of the roses, the beautifully photographed images, and the descriptions of fragrances and growing habits brought the colourful characters in the catalogues to life in Sophia's imagination. The Old-World roses were present alongside new releases, there were climbers, ramblers, floribundas, hybrid teas, standards, bush roses, weeping standards, and miniatures – such abundance and diversity. The Gardener was perusing the other catalogues and jotting down notes in his little brown notebook. Every now and then he would stop and scratch his head with the end of his pencil stub and stare out into space, no doubt conjuring up his future garden in his mind.

'Sophia, why don't you pick out a rose of your own to plant in the garden, something for you to nurture and observe throughout the seasons.'

'Oh, thank you,' Sophia murmured, suddenly feeling a little uncertain, wondering if her garden visits would continue. The Gardener must have sensed how Sophia was feeling as he quoted Audrey Hepburn.

'To plant a garden is to believe in tomorrow.'

'I saw a rose in the catalogue called Many Happy Returns, perhaps I could plant that one?' Sophia asked, feeling a little brighter.

'Sounds good to me!' the Gardener enthused.

Two weeks later the bare-rooted roses arrived. Sophia was excited when she saw the box, but when she opened it and saw bare twigs and roots, hardly knowing what was up and what was down, she was suddenly filled with dread.

Thankfully, the Gardener appeared, and seeing Sophia's wide eyes and scared rabbit look, he sprang into action.

'Getting a bare-rooted rose started is amazingly easy. It may just look like a dead stick, but here in your hands you have something that is bursting with life and just waiting to awaken. A bare-rooted rose is like a fairy tale; the sleeping princess awakes, and we can make this miracle occur. Anyone who is jaded, blasé, or tired of life needs to witness what is going to happen here. It is just the most exciting, life-affirming, wondrous thing! Let us get started, shall we?'

Sophia moved a little closer, not wanting to miss a moment of this spectacle. Her sense of dread had been replaced by a breathless anticipation.

'First, I'll need half a bucket of water and some of the seaweed solution to help with the root development.'

Sophia filled up a heavy galvanised iron bucket at the tank and the Gardener added a small capful of a brown liquid and swirled it around with a stick, making the water look like a strong cup of tea.

'Now we submerge the roots completely, but we keep the bud union and the branches of the rose above the water line. The rose can sit in the water overnight, and we can plant the rose tomorrow morning, as you said you are calling in.'

Using a garden fork, the Gardener started to fork the soil, making a hole. Sophia had thought he would use a spade, but remembered his story about the earthworms. As if reading her mind, the Gardener explained further.

'I'm using a fork to make the edges of the hole rough so that the roots will head out into the soil easily, rather than growing around and around the edges of a neat hole which can stunt the plant's growth. And as you know, I don't want to slice through any worms who aerate and enrich the soil for the roses.'

When he had dug a hole about 40 centimetres wide and 30 centimetres deep, the Gardener took a small handful of seaweed pellets and put them in a mound at the bottom of the hole and then covered them in soil, creating a cone-shaped mound. Sophia wondered what on earth he was doing. Taking the rose plant, the Gardener said, 'Let us have a look at the roots. Now, go carefully here, but we need to trim off any that are damaged or curling or too long. When we put the rose in the hole we want the roots to sit neatly over this mound I have created, and we need the mound to be the right height so that when we fill in the hole the bud union of the rose will be about an inch above the soil.'

Sophia examined the roots and gently made a few adjustments before handing the rose back to the Gardener.

'No, no, you can do this. I mustn't have all the fun,' the Gardener smiled.

And Sophia did, too, testing the height of the mound and spreading out the roots. The Gardener backfilled the hole halfway, and then he filled the hole with water and they both watched it drain away.

'Roses like a good draining soil and hate to have wet roots, so the rose is going to be happy here.'

He continued to fill the hole and then pressed down the soil around the crown of the roses firmly with the toe of his boot, creating a well around the rose. He then let Sophia give the rose a final deep watering and they stood back to admire their work.

'We can just trim off any damaged tips of the rose canes to an outward facing bud, and the rest is up to the rose.'

When Sophia decided to walk to the garden that morning, the sun had just popped over the horizon and was basking in a strip of apricot sky under a blanket of soft grey clouds.

She had barely taken a couple of steps when she felt a few spots of rain sparkle on her cheeks. She had her little woollen hat on so she didn't feel the rain on her head. She kept walking, unperturbed, as the few drops became a light shower. She laughed to herself as the rain hit her eyelashes, enjoying the sensation. No one else seemed to be around, and she enjoyed having the world to herself for a moment. She had not thought to bring an umbrella; she did not even have a bag with her, and that made her feel free and light-hearted.

A few magpies joined her, seeming excited at the prospect of softer soil and perhaps a juicy worm rearing its head. The plants seemed to be nodding their heads as the raindrops bounced on their leaves. For that moment Sophia felt very content to be walking in the rain, so she did not speed up; in fact, she moved along at a dreamy pace. The rain started to get heavier just as Sophia came into the presence of a large old flowering gum tree. The path under the tree was dry and she felt the invitation to wait under the tree until the rain eased. She stood with her back to the trunk and her hands on the rough bark, and was struck by a strong feeling of warmth and support from the tree. She could feel the strength, stability, and vitality of the tree, and felt that she was being embraced by it and accepted unconditionally. As the rain continued to come down at the periphery of the tree's canopy, she felt rooted to the spot, contented, and began to feel a very unfamiliar sense of belonging.

After a while the rain began to ease, and Sophia could see patches of blue sky. Breathing easily, she marvelled at the experience she had just been given. When she could see no more raindrops in the puddles, she left the shelter of the tree and with a backward glance filled with deep gratitude to the tree, she continued into the garden knowing that she was making progress in finding her way in the world.

Spring Returns

Spring returned to the garden with such enthusiasm, mirroring the way Sophia felt when she saw the bare rosebushes she had so painstakingly pruned with the Gardener spring into life.

The first leaves to appear surprised Sophia with their colours; lime green, deep burgundy, russet red, and cool maroon. And Sophia was amazed when the Gardener explained to her that the colourful first offerings of the roses were less palatable to predators, giving the roses a head start and a chance to get established before they were subjected to any pest attack. The leaves, so fresh and clean and abundant, were a stark contrast to the yellow spotted sparse leaves that said farewell in Winter.

Peering out over the garden, it looked to Sophia like the rose bushes had shrugged on colourful knitted cardigans and were standing around chatting at a country market. The tips of some of the rose shoots showed the swelling of the first signs of buds. Even though Sophia was witnessing her first transition from Winter to Spring in the garden, she had no doubts that life would return to the garden and that did not lessen her excitement now.

Sophia also realised that the extreme joy she felt was the result of having seen the dark, barren, lifeless, still garden in Winter.

Sophia put her heavy grocery bags down on the ground to rearrange the handles. Looking up, a notice on the community noticeboard caught her attention.

Rosenhaven Park
Garden Volunteers Wanted,
No Experience Necessary,
All Welcome,
Tuesdays 8am-12noon.

Sophia knew the park and had often walked through there on her way to the train station, usually in the late afternoon, so had never seen anyone working there. People from a nearby nursing home were often escorted there to sit under the shady trees and to admire the colourful plantings and the joyful squeaks of the rainbow lorikeets announcing the arrival of the blossom on the flowering gum trees.

'No experience necessary. All welcome,' she read aloud.

Sophia woke up to an overcast but otherwise fine morning remembering that she was going to Rosenhaven Park to join the volunteers, feeling both a little bit nervous and a touch excited. She packed her gardening tools, gloves, and hat into her bag and walked down the stairs and out the back entrance so she would not have to talk to anyone.

Slightly underestimating the time it would take to get to the garden, Sophia was a little bit late and hoped it wouldn't matter. Well, it certainly did not seem to. She was welcomed with open arms and introduced to lots of people whose names she wouldn't be able to recall, although some of them wore nametags which was helpful. She signed her name and time of arrival in the logbook and was given a high visibility vest to put on.

Sophia was allocated a garden bed to work on with two other ladies who regaled her with stories of their long and interesting lives whilst they weeded, trimmed, and tidied up. The time passed very quickly and before long someone was ringing the morning tea bell. Sophia sat with her new friends, happy to watch them greeting and chatting with all their other friends, not feeling the need to reveal anything about herself. The conversation drifted from cuttings, seedlings, and garden pests to recent operations, exploits of grandchildren and wayward husbands, and was intermingled with words of wisdom.

'To survive old age, you need to have fortitude,' and it appeared they did. Sophia was filled with admiration for these people, some of whom had no gardens of their own, much like herself, but still needed a connection with the earth, and she could see how their connection with the other volunteers was as strong as their love of the plants. As Sophia packed up her tools and thanked her garden companions for an enjoyable morning, she felt grateful and privileged to have been warmly welcomed into this special community. With dirt under her fingernails and aching muscles, Sophia returned home feeling contented.

Sophia shoved her letters into her overflowing bag and headed out of the front door onto the busy street, narrowly avoiding colliding with a delivery man. The front of one of her letters caught her eye. It was her lease renewal.

'No,' she said out loud, shaking her head as if trying to dislodge a very unpleasant thought, 'no way.' Just about to stride off, Sophia glanced down and was surprised to see a butterfly on the concrete footpath opening and shutting its wings. Before anyone could step on it, she bent down and ushered it gently onto her hand. She could feel the tickle of its tiny feet on her fingertips. Sophia looked around to see where she could release it. The butterfly spotted it before she did and took off in the direction of a nectar rich grevillea hanging over a nearby fence. As Sophia watched the butterfly in flight, she understood what she must do.

In no time she was standing in front of the real estate agent's window and she knew exactly what she was looking for. A peaceful garden, preferably with a small cottage attached. Most of the images were of square concrete blocks with synthetic turf, multiple cars parked on paved front yards, and maybe a yucca, if you were lucky. But there was one image in the corner way down low where you could just see the outline of a building hidden behind a hedge and an overgrown cottage garden – and yes, there were a few roses poking their heads over the side fence. Feeling calm and in control Sophia confidently walked up the three steps and pulled open the heavy glass door.

The first thing she noticed as she stepped inside was the floral arrangement on the reception desk: pale pink hothouse roses accompanied by fronds of soft silvery grey foliage in an elegant ceramic bowl.

'How can we help you today?' the receptionist asked pleasantly.

'I'm looking for a new place to live,' she replied without a second thought.

'Well, come on in and take a seat. I was just about to make a cup of tea, would you like one?'

Sophia left the office an hour later with a list of properties to inspect and tendrils of hope taking root in her heart.

The Gardener sat in the potting shed alone, not that that was unusual. He looked down at his calloused hands and the dirt under his fingernails. Spread out in front of him was the plan of the garden, his masterplan. So much of it had been completed and he was well pleased. There was one section that needed attention, an older part of the garden that led out to a flower meadow.

The Gardener sighed. Did he have the energy to take on this new project? And what would it be this time? His vision of the garden had never failed him before.

Where is Sophia? he wondered. *She could help me.*

The Gardener got slowly to his feet and walked over to the door, propped himself against the frame, and stared out into the distance. Then he saw her zig-zagging through the roses. Smiling to himself, he thought, *I won't put the kettle on yet, looks like she will be quite a while.* The Gardener eased himself down onto the creaky bench on the verandah and let his thoughts wander back to the first day Sophia had visited the garden.

He could clearly see her in his mind's eye, all hesitation and confusion and that black cloud that hung over her, but to see her now made his heart glad. Of all the people who had passed through the garden over the long years, Sophia was the one who stood out. No one else had been able to see the beauty and the wonder of the roses like she did, and only Sophia knew the mystery that was hidden in the rose. And the Gardener, though he did not want to admit it, felt old as he sat there watching Sophia make her way towards him.

She had seen him now, and waved enthusiastically. He stood up, shaking off his melancholy thoughts and went out to meet her.

'Good to see you, Sophia,' he said in his familiar cheery voice. 'I have an interesting project to discuss with you.'

Sophia knocked on the door of the potting shed with her elbow, balancing the cake tin in one hand, and the bag of books in the other. The Gardener opened the door as if he had been waiting for her.

'Ah, Sophia, here you are at last. I thought you had abandoned me.'

'No, no, of course not,' Sophia spluttered hastily, and the Gardener laughed.

'It's alright, Sophia, I am just teasing you. I knew you would come back and see me, but I did not know you would bring cake. I think I'd better put the kettle on,' he said relieving her of the old-fashioned cake tin.

'I've missed this,' Sophia said wistfully, sinking down into her usual seat, 'what a crazy time we've been having.'

'You can say that again,' the Gardener said, placing the tea tray down on the coffee table. 'But what have you learnt, Sophia? Unusual circumstances make the best teachers.'

'What have I learnt?' Sophia pondered, her eyes looking way off into the distance. 'That life is unpredictable, that's for sure, but I guess we already knew that.'

'Yes,' the Gardener agreed, 'but even though we know it, most people live their lives as if everything is always going to stay the same, and then when a major shift happens they find that they can't cope and things start to fall apart. But if we really see life as constantly changing, just like in the rose garden, then we appreciate the present moment so much more, and we are ready to adapt and embrace whatever the future has in store for us. And if we constantly nourish and build our inner world – tend the garden within, if you will – then we always have rich reserves of energy, inspiration, and contentment to draw upon in times of need.'

Sophia smiled, she knew exactly what he meant, and gently tuning into her relaxed breathing she could feel a warm glow of peace throughout her entire body.

'So,' the Gardener said, 'what about this cake?'

It seemed strange that Sophia had never noticed the ivy-covered archway in one of the walls of the garden.

Through the narrow keyhole opening she could see out to a vast meadow, gently undulating with golden grasses and wildflowers stretching way out into the distance. Sophia could sense the contrast between the darker controlled world inside the confines of the garden and the wide-open spaces beyond.

For Sophia, the garden was the place she retreated to, but now she could feel a stirring inside her that perhaps she was ready, was confident enough, to move out into the big wide world; almost like hatching out of an egg. She loved the garden and the sense of strength and security it gave her, but there was something alluring about the sense of freedom out in the meadow.

A gentle breeze was rustling the soft grasses and wispy clouds were drifting across a blue sky. There were no pathways through the meadow, the ground looked as if it could be uneven.

Is it safe to go out? Sophia wondered. *The sunshine is warm ... perhaps I could make a few tentative steps out there, but would I be able to find my way back to the garden or find my way home?*

Sophia admitted to herself that she felt fearful of this great open space, but at the same time she could feel an unfamiliar yet persistent force pulling her in that direction.

'I know what I must do,' Sophia decided, rummaging through her gardening basket for the ball of fine garden twine she carried around with her. Tying the end of the ball of twine to an old brass hook she found halfway up the wall and holding the string firmly, Sophia consciously put one foot in front of the other and walked out into the beautiful meadow.

Sophia could hear hammering as she approached the garden.

What could be happening? she wondered. Rounding the corner, she detected the source of the noise, a workman in a high visibility vest was boarding up the gate. Sophia broke into a sprint.

'What's going on? What are you doing? I'm just going into the garden now,' Sophia panted out, panic rising.

'No, you're not,' he said gruffly. 'The garden's closed, the old shed's an asbestos hazard and is being pulled down, and this overrun old garden hasn't been open to the public for years. It will be gone soon anyway, once the developers move in.'

Sophia stared – no, she glared at him with disbelief, and then she took a deep breath and a step back, but kept facing the workman. Then in a slow but firm voice, Sophia spoke to him, looking him straight in the eye.

'The shed is not a hazard, it's in perfect condition and it's made of stone, and the garden is certainly not overrun – I've worked in it all year, and it's practically manicured.' Sophia was amazed at how steady and strong she felt.

'If you've been in the garden you've been trespassing, and if you've been in that shed, you're a damned fool,' he spat back at her.

At that very moment, a white feather drifted down on the breeze between them. Sophia took a deep breath, smiled, and calmly said, 'Oh, you've got the wrong garden. Come with me, I'll show you.' She grabbed the workman's sleeve and pulled him. The shock of her touching him was like a zap of electricity, and he came along with her as she commanded, not uttering a word of protest.

Sophia soon found the hidden door with the rose brass handle which opened smoothly, and she ushered the workman inside and closed the door behind them.

'Follow me,' she said brightly, as if leading a behind-the-hedges garden tour, and soon they were at the top of the Grand Promenade. Her beautiful garden was laid out before them, fragrant and in full bloom.

The workman looked as if his legs were about to buckle, so Sophia grabbed his arm again and motioned him towards the bench under the Pierre de Ronsard climber. At that point, precisely on cue, Michael began to play his harp.

'Well, knock me down with a feather,' the workman said. 'They must have sent me to the wrong garden.'

Sophia pushed open the brass rose door handle and entered the garden, the dappled light a patterned carpet beneath her feet. The roses were blooming abundantly and the mild morning air was filled with fragrance.

Sophia meandered slowly along the neat pathways, stopping and admiring blooms along the way. When she arrived at the Rose Pavilion, she saw the Gardener and the older Sophia, heads together in conversation. She smiled at them indulgently as they talked and laughed. She found herself a seat away from them and sat down to watch. Even though she did not know what they were talking about, just to observe the comfortable way they were with each other made the younger Sophia feel deeply satisfied and at ease. Sophia closed her eyes and let the feeling of deep peace wash over her, and she knew that this was how she was supposed to feel.

At last the struggle was over. She had no doubts, and her heart was filled with joy and contentment. Sophia was completely confident that she was where she was supposed to be, and that all would be well.

Gently opening her eyes, Sophia was not surprised to see that she was alone. Feeling relaxed and strong, she picked up her bags and made her way out of the garden. In her hand, the key to her new home felt cool and smooth.

Closing the heavy door behind her with a wooden thud, Sophia went out into the world and her new reality.

The packing boxes were still spilling their contents onto the floor when Sophia awoke to sunlight filtering through the lace curtains. The world seemed comfortingly quiet, apart from one bird making a joyful sound.

Sophia slipped out of bed and pulled on her abstract floral silk kimono, and tiptoed to the sliding door that led out to the garden. She had not unpacked her gardening clogs yet, so stepped barefoot onto her tiny patch of lawn still damp with morning dew.

A shiver went through her, not from cold, but from absolute pleasure to be standing in her own small garden. It needed a lot of tender loving care but already it was her little piece of paradise. Secateurs in hand, she drifted down to where the small collection of roses were elbowing their way out from tall grass and leggy geraniums. So glad that she had moved house in Spring, she was able to pick a bunch of fragrant roses of varying shades of pink to take inside to enjoy.

Sophia closed her eyes and breathed in deeply. Could anything be more perfect than this? Answering herself, she knew it could.

Must go in and put on the kettle.

> *'The world is full of magic things patiently waiting*
> *for our senses to grow sharper.'*
> **~ W.B. Yeats**

Acknowledgments

Heartfelt thanks to Blaise van Hecke and the team at Busybird Publishing who helped me take a seed of an idea and make it flourish, and for facilitating the inspirational Busybird Writing Retreat on the magical island of Bali in October 2019 where my random thoughts finally fell into place.

A warm thank you to the exceptionally talented Deborah O'Brien for her constant friendship and quiet encouragement, and giving me an insight into the inspiring world of a dedicated author.

Many thanks must go to the loyal readers of my *Art, Gardens and Always Roses* monthly newsletter who are spread far and wide across the globe, and constantly remind me that somewhere in the world there are always roses in bloom.

Thank you too to my many Rose Society friends, both near and far, for their interest and enthusiasm.

Deep gratitude to friends and family past and present for their influence and inspiration. My world is richer because of them.

And finally, extra special thanks to my bookworm husband, Brian, for his steadfast support.

About the Author

Michelle Endersby is a writer and visual artist from Melbourne, Australia.

She was the winner of the inaugural Audrey Daybook Short Story Prize in 2019 with her endearing tale, *The Caretaker*.

Inspired by a vision of a light-filled rose garden she experienced on awakening from a coma following emergency brain surgery, Michelle is enthusiastic about growing, photographing, painting, and writing about roses.

Michelle is the creator of the popular monthly *Art, Gardens and Always Roses* email newsletter.

www.michelleendersbyart.com